BETWEEN HEAVEN AND EARTH

BOOK 2
IN THE ANGEL CHRONICLES SERIES

BY
ESTER LÓPEZ

Published by Writing & Photographic Services, LLC
https://www.facebook.com/WPSLLCPublisher/

Between Heaven and Earth

Cover design and interior by ebooklaunch.com

ISBN 978-0-9970033-6-9

To keep up to date on the author's book releases, and to
Get the FREE "Vaedra Chronicles" companion book,
Please join Ester's Readers Group at
www.esterlopez.com

Follow Ester's Blogs at:
www.esterlopez.com
and
www.AuthorBlogSpot.esterlopez.com

Follow Ester on:
www.Facebook.com/EsterLopezAuthor

And if you like the story, please leave an honest review at
Amazon.com or Goodreads.com

For my sister Susan, who is the inspiration for the character
Susan Santos.

CHAPTER ONE

María Rojas looked up and down the alley to make sure no one watched before sliding the lid open and peering inside her favorite dumpster.

Good. No rats.

She scrunched her nose as the faint, pungent aroma of rotting food assaulted her senses. Her dumpster had once been used by neighboring restaurants, although lately it had been taken over by local offices for paper trash. But it was an odor she could live with, considering her choices.

Pushing off from the sturdy can beside the large metal container, she hauled herself up through the opening and dropped onto a pile of cardboard boxes broken down inside the dumpster.

She had slept in worse places, but tonight she would sleep well.

She made the sign of the cross and whispered her nightly prayer.

"Angel of God, my guardian dear, to whom God's love commits me here, ever this day be at my side, to light, to guard, to rule and guide. Amen."

Making the sign of the cross once more, she curled up on the cardboard pallet and covered her face with her hat.

Early October, the nights cooled down in Pensacola. She hugged herself to keep warm. If she didn't get off the streets soon, the nights would become unbearably cold.

Patting the outside of her coat, she made certain her earnings were still inside. Tomorrow, after work, she would make a deposit.

One day soon she would have enough money saved to pay off Mr. Turner and get her apartment and belongings back. Then she would see about returning to nursing school. Her instructors gave her incompletes to finish the term, but she would have to make up all those classes before moving on.

Even with the extra hours Mr. Brodsky had given her at the Greasy Spoon, the pay wasn't enough to get her out of debt. Maybe he would let her become a server as well as dishwasher. With her skills, she had limited choices. She forced the thoughts from her mind, and gradually dozed off.

• • •

Hours later, she awoke to the sound of footsteps running down the alley toward her.

"Hey, old man, what's your hurry?" a male voice called out.

Her pulse quickened as she sat up and listened. Peering through a rust hole in the dumpster, she saw three men. One of them was someone she had seen at the Soup Kitchen. The three men were about the same six feet in height.

She moved closer to get a better look. Although two of them had their backs to her, she saw from the street light they wore blue jeans with casual suit jackets. One man had on running shoes with a lightning bolt design on the side. The other man wore loafers.

She recognized the old man as Joe Blue, when he threw his hands up in the air. "I don't want any trouble," he said. His eyes widened, a worried look on his face.

Her heart rate shot up. *That didn't sound good. Oh, Lord, help him.*

"It's too late for that, old man. You've already seen too much," the man in the running shoes said.

The other man reached into his pocket, pulled out a taser and stuck Joe with it. Joe jerked a few times then fell back against the wall before sliding to the ground.

She leaned closer to the side of the dumpster and saw the man in the running shoes pull a hypodermic needle out of his pocket.

He pulled back on the syringe, while inserting the needle into a bottle.

The other man held Joe's arm while the first one injected him with the liquid.

"N—," she tried to scream, but her vocal chords wouldn't cooperate.

Panic set in. She had to stop them. She brought her hand up to hit the inside of the dumpster, when someone clamped a hand over her mouth and pulled her back, pinning her arms to her sides. Startled, she jerked, banging the wall of her makeshift sleeping quarters with her foot. Then a leg wrapped over her hips, preventing her from moving. Her heart pounded furiously.

The two men turned and looked at the dumpster. Her heart skipped a beat as she held her breath. *Don't come over here.*

Two rats scurried out the top of the container.

Wincing at the sight, she swallowed hard.

*Where did **they** come from? And who was holding her?*

She struggled to free herself when a sense of peace flowed through her suddenly, as if she, too, had been injected with something potent.

"Damn rats," one of the men said.

"They give me the creeps," the other one said, turning back to Joe.

"What about him?"

"We'll take him with us. I know just the place to leave him." He bent down and picked up Joe under the shoulders.

"Grab his feet."

Where were they going with Joe Blue?

The hand against her mouth loosened, as well as the arm around her waist and the leg over her hip. The warmth of the body behind her left immediately. She pulled away and spun around on her side to see who shared the small quarters with her. In the dark, she made out the shape of a man, much larger than her small five-foot-two-inch frame, with hair that hung down below his ears.

"How…did you get in here?" she asked.

"Never mind that, we have to leave now," he said. He ran a hand through his hair. He stood up, put his hands on the top of the dumpster and leapt over the side of the container.

María may have seen three men tonight, but he had seen six, counting the two evil spirits, the two criminals, the old man and his Guardian Angel.

The spirits were so intent on their evil deed they failed to notice his presence, or they would have alerted the two moles.

He held his hands up to help María down from the top of the container.

"Hey!" She leaned over the edge. "How did you make that jump in one movement?" She hiked a leg over the side.

He caught her under the armpits and pulled her toward him. Her hands pressed against his shoulders as he slowly brought her to the ground. She was light and pleasing to hold and the touch of her hands against his bare skin felt warm and comforting.

Earlier, when he had his hand across her mouth, her lips felt soft and her warm breath moistened his fingers. The sensation that ran through him when he cradled her body against his was unexpected, but he remembered it from before.

Before? If he had never manifested in the flesh, how could he remember that strange and pleasant sensation? Now, he would never forget it.

María scratched her head as she looked him up and down. A smile escaped his lips when he noticed how she tried to look mad.

"Who are you and what were you doing in my dumpster?" María demanded, her hands on her hips.

"Your dumpster? I thought it belonged to the City of Pensacola." He turned and walked away from her. He had forgotten how amusing she could be, but he had to get her to safety before the thugs returned.

"I asked you a question," she demanded, following him.

"The name's Mike," he said over his shoulder, and quickened his pace. Hopefully, she would follow without further questions.

"Hey, wait up. What happened to Joe Blue?" She trotted after him.

"They took his body. They'll dump it under the overpass for someone to find in the morning." María's inquisitiveness never ceased to entertain him.

"How do you *know* that?" she asked, taking longer strides to keep up.

"I know a lot of things." He stopped and turned toward her. "Right now, we need to leave this place." He could hear the car slowly moving toward them.

"But shouldn't we call the cops or something?" she protested.

"It wouldn't do any good. The man is dead, and his spirit moved on. They wouldn't believe you anyway, because you don't know where the body is."

"Well…if you know, couldn't you tell them?" she said, poking his chest.

"They can't see me. Only you can see me."

"What are you talking about?" She put her hands on her hips and looked up at him.

The car moved closer to the alley, as the sound of rubber tires crushing against asphalt grew louder. He reached his arms around María and held her tight. The sensation of her body against his stunned him momentarily, but he thought of the Waffle House and was there instantly.

• • •

"How did you…we…get here?" She craned her neck to look up at this amazingly good-looking guy.

"I'll explain everything," he said, releasing her. He held the door of the Waffle House open as she walked past him and went inside. Immediately, she missed the warmth of his touch.

Who was this guy, and why did she feel safe around him?

Inside, there were two people in a booth, as well as a waitress and a cook. Dazed, she found a booth on the far side of the restaurant, near a window, and slipped into the seat. The man sat across from her.

"Okay, who are you, and why are we here?" she asked. Looking at him, she crossed her arms over her chest. He had a lot to answer for, that was certain.

Handsome in an elegant sort of way, he looked nothing like any of the men she had seen on campus. His dark-brown eyes and golden-brown skin had a healthy glow. His black, thick brows, matching his wavy hair, drew her to his face, but the dimple on his left cheek held her gaze. He was gorgeous.

Oh, and those muscular shoulders and bear arms had seen a lot of workouts. His forearms were covered with black curly hair and his full lips and round nose made him look like a guy who enjoyed life and knew how to have fun.

"Hey, there. My name's Susan. Can I get you both something to drink?" The waitress interrupted her thoughts. Susan was in her forties with thick, grayish-brown hair pulled back in a pony tail with bangs.

Mike's gaze snapped toward the woman.

"Can you see me?" he asked her, his eyes wide.

"Of course, I can see you, honey, I'm not blind." She lowered her bifocals. "And you're not bad-looking either," she said, putting her hands on her hips. "What in the world are you two wearing?" Susan looked them both over.

"Um…we've been to a costume party," María lied. She was just as anxious to find out why Mike was wearing an ancient Roman soldier's uniform, complete with a breastplate. Although, her reason for wearing a man's suit was to hide the fact she was a woman living on the streets, she wasn't about to tell a stranger that.

Mike looked at her and raised an eyebrow.

"You know, you look really familiar somehow. Have you been in here before?" Susan asked him, in a raspy voice.

"I don't think so," Mike said, looking at Susan. "This is my first time here."

"I'm pretty bad at remembering names, but I sure can remember a face. And I've seen you in here before."

Mike leaned back and managed to smile. "Maybe I have a twin somewhere," he said.

"Was your father on the police force?" Susan asked, looking down at him.

"My father? Uh, no…I…no." Mike shook his head slowly, then sat back in his seat.

"Hmmm," Susan said, chewing on the end of her pen. Her tired greenish-brown eyes studied him.

"Could we have some coffee with cream and sugar, please?" Mike asked.

"Sure, honey. I'll be right back." She turned and left.

María leaned forward and whispered loudly, "I thought you said no one could see you?"

"Well, I've never manifested in the flesh before. I didn't think anyone could see me," he said, closing his eyes. Then he disappeared.

"Hey, where'd he go?" Susan asked, setting down the coffee and creamer.

"Um…bathroom," María lied, chewing on her bottom lip.

Susan looked around, then pulled out her pad and pen. "Are you ready to order, honey?"

"Not yet. Maybe in a few minutes," she said.

"Okay. I'll check back, then." Susan returned to the grill area.

"Can you see me now?" Mike asked.

"No, but I can hear you." María reached across the table and moved her hand through the space he had just occupied. "How are you doing that?"

Mike reappeared and caught her hand in his. "I'm your Guardian Angel."

She yanked her hand away and dropped back into her seat. "What?"

Mike leaned across the table and spoke in a whisper. "I've been your Guardian Angel since the day you were born."

María's mouth dropped open. A million questions formed in her mind instantly. "Am I going to die?" Her heart rate shot up at the thought.

"Yes, but not for a very long time." Mike leaned forward. "You were about to scream when you witnessed that murder. It wasn't your time to go, so I had to intervene, or you would have been next."

She caught her throat with her hand. "I…couldn't scream. I tried but—" She remembered the scene vividly.

"I stopped you, then realized you were going to bang on the dumpster. I had to take drastic measures. My mission is to protect you from all harm."

"How did you know I was going to bang on the dumpster?"

"I can hear your thoughts."

María blinked as her hand dropped away from her throat. "All of them?"

Mike nodded. "Since the day you were born."

She swallowed hard, recalling her recent thoughts about him. "Can you turn it off?"

"I'm afraid not."

She had a lot of thoughts—questions—running through her mind. "When do you have to…go back?"

"Go back?" he asked, raising an eyebrow.

"You know, to heaven?"

"I guess when it's your time to go. I'm with you for the long haul."

"You mean until I die?"

Mike nodded.

"Well, are you two ready to order?" Maria jumped at Susan's approach.

"Hi." He smiled at Susan. "I guess I'll have the All-Star Special."

Susan scribbled on her pad, then froze. She looked at Mike. "You used to be a regular here." She pointed at him with her pen. "And you used to sit at this same booth and ordered the same thing every time you came in. I remember now." Susan turned and called out. "Bobby, come here."

The cook approached the table, wiping his hands on his apron. Mike looked at Maria and offered a half smile, raising an eyebrow.

"Look at him, Bobby. Who does he remind you of?"

Bobby stared at Mike. "You look like the cop who used to come in here with his partner every Sunday while on patrol." Bobby turned toward Susan. "But that was—"

"Twenty-three years ago." Susan finished.

"You must have me confused with someone else," Mike said.

"Your partner still comes in here from time to time. I'll ask him," Susan said.

"That's a good idea," Mike said, raising both eyebrows. "Now, how about that special?"

"One All-Star Special coming up. How about you, honey, do you want anything to eat?" Susan looked at María.

"I...uh...I'll have the same thing, please," she said, looking at Susan.

"I'll be right back," Susan said, pushing Bobby back toward the kitchen.

She glanced at the clock. It was after four a.m. She would have to be at work in a couple of hours. She felt for her pocket with the cash in it.

"I hate to ask this, but who's paying for this meal?" She poured the creamer into her cup of coffee.

"You'll have to, since I don't carry any money," Mike said, taking a sip of his coffee.

"You know how long I've been saving?" She stirred in the sugar. It had been two months since she had been locked out of her apartment.

"Yes, and if you hadn't dropped out of college, you would have made a lot more money in the near future."

María glared at him. "Where were you when I had to make that decision?" With no place to live, where was she supposed to go? Mr. Turner had everything she owned in storage, including her books. She had no money to replace them, let alone pay her back rent.

"I tried to guide you in the other direction, but you didn't listen."

María sipped her coffee. How could she have done otherwise? After her father's untimely death from cancer two years earlier had drained their savings, her mother was forced to sell the only home Maria had ever known to pay off his debt. Without her mother's income, she had no place to live, and no way to continue school. "Well, maybe you didn't try hard enough."

Mike put his coffee down. "What is that supposed to mean?"

"How long have you been an angel, anyway? Did you have any other assignments before you were my Guardian Angel?"

"I…honestly don't remember," he said, sipping his coffee.

"Here you go," Susan said, setting the All-Star Specials down in front of them. "I'll get you some more coffee." She turned back to the kitchen.

"Wow, that's a lot of food," María said. She hadn't eaten this much food in a long time…since her mother had been well.

"Eat up. You won't get to eat again until late today, remember?" Mike said.

Susan returned with the coffee and poured some for her. She turned to pour some for Mike. "I thought you wanted cream and sugar?" she asked him, looking at his half-full cup.

"No, I drink mine black," he said.

"That's right." Susan nodded as she locked gazes with Mike, then left.

"How do you know you drink your coffee black?" María asked him. "Have you ever had coffee before? And do angels eat and drink?"

"I…no…angels don't eat and drink, unless we take human form."

"Well, the way you said it was like you'd been drinking coffee for years. How do you know you won't like it with cream and sugar?"

"I don't, I mean…I like mine black."

"Yeah, right." She poked her eggs with her fork. She couldn't understand why she wanted to be mad at this man. He hadn't done anything wrong to deserve her anger. This was the first hot breakfast she'd had in a week and it tasted good, but the cost would set her back on reaching her goal.

Mike watched her eat while new thoughts ran through his head. He took another sip of coffee. The smells and tastes that he experienced sent thousands of images through his mind. Images of things he remembered from a past that he didn't know he had. And her questions brought new thoughts to his mind as well. For instance, the first taste of coffee felt so natural to his tongue, yet he remembered tasting coffee that was too strong as well as too weak. He remembered coffee that was exquisite as well as downright nasty. But if this was his first taste, then where did these memories come from? And how did he know he liked it black?

Mike tasted the eggs. Boy, they were good. He really missed this breakfast. His hand froze over the sausage.

How could he miss something he never had? And why did it taste so familiar? The hash browns were good and crispy, just the way he liked them. But how did he know that?

He cut his sausage patties up and folded them into his last slice of toast and made a sandwich out of it. He stared at the food in his hand. This was all so familiar to him. Did he actually come here with a partner as Susan suggested? Had he been a cop at one time? And why did he even pick this place? María had never come here before, and how did he know this place was even here?

"So now what happens?" María asked, finishing her last piece of toast.

"We wait until you have to be at work."

"That's not for another hour and a half," she said, glancing at the clock. "What do we do in the meantime?" She sat back in her seat, her arms crossed over her chest.

"I can answer any questions you might have," he said.

"Really?"

He nodded.

"What else do angels do besides read people's minds?"

"We protect and guard you, give guidance, in other words, everything you pray and ask us to do, providing it's God's will for you, but I can't interfere with free will."

"Can you see into the future…my future?"

"Sometimes."

"Well…what does mine look like?"

"Your destiny was to become a nurse, but you changed that with your decision to drop out of college."

"Why didn't you help me with that decision? You know why I made it." She pointed at him as she lowered her voice.

He had tried desperately to convince her to stay in school, but her mother's death pulled her away from logical thinking. "Yes, I know why, but you didn't ask for my help then. You made that decision on your own." María hadn't been tuned in to listening to her conscience, which was his only way of speaking to her as a spirit being.

María leaned her head back against the booth and closed her eyes.

"You had options," he continued. He knew she couldn't see those options at the time.

"Yeah, like what?" She straightened in her seat.

"You could've talked to a counselor. You were on a scholarship. They could have helped you find financing so you could keep your apartment."

"It's too late," she moaned.

"No, it's not. Call them. You could get back in next semester," he urged. If only she would listen to him now.

"I asked for an incomplete in all my classes before the funeral. I couldn't concentrate enough to study for the finals."

"I know." María did need time to grieve. She had no one to confide in at the time, either. Her mother had just given up the fight with pneumonia. She longed to be with her husband, but he couldn't explain that to María.

María closed her eyes and inhaled deeply, letting her breath out slowly through her mouth.

Her mother had been a nurse and ever since she was a little girl, she had wanted to be one, too, but her circumstances had changed with her mother's recent death. The money had simply run out.

She opened her eyes. Living on the streets had become dangerous. There were too many things going on lately that scared her, and tonight was the worst.

"Promise me you'll call them," Mike said softly, his brows raised with hopeful anticipation.

She looked at him, at those piercing brown eyes. How could she say no? "I promise." She looked down at her hands, folded on the table. Her initial thoughts of Mike came to mind. "You, uh, didn't hear what I had been thinking earlier, did you?"

"Of course I did." He set his coffee down and pinned her with an intense look, then he winked.

She tensed her jaws and felt her cheeks grow hot.

He smiled at her. There was something so sexy about the way he looked at her, it threw her off guard. No one had ever looked at her that way.

You are a very beautiful young woman. She heard his voice in her head, an audible sound.

"Yeah, right," she mumbled. "A woman who sleeps in dumpsters and wears over-sized men's suits?"

He crossed his arms over his chest. *You could change all that, you know.* His voice was audible again, but only in her mind.

"Why haven't you shown yourself to me before?"

"It wasn't necessary until now," Mike said.

She thought of all the times she had felt lonely and could have used a friend. She lowered her head and sipped her coffee. "So, after tonight, do you disappear again... forever?" The thought saddened her. She glanced up into his eyes.

"If you want me to, I will."

"No! I…mean, I like your company. Don't go." She lowered her eyes once more.

"I'll always be here, whether you see me or not," he said.

"Yes, but I wouldn't be able to talk to you," she said, gazing into his dark brown eyes.

"Of course you can talk to me," he said, touching her forearm.

The warmth from his hand ran throughout her body instantaneously, like someone turned the heat up with the flick of a wrist.

"I wouldn't be able to hear you, though, would I?"

"If you pay attention, you can hear me when I speak to your mind."

"What about Joe Blue? I need to tell someone about what happened, don't I?" she whispered.

"Yes, but it can wait until later this morning. The police will find him and make a report. You'll be able to fill in the missing pieces for them later."

"Were you an angel when you were a…cop?" She sipped her coffee but didn't move the arm he was touching. She drew comfort from his nearness.

Mike glanced away momentarily, then back at her. "No. I…was…I don't remember being a cop. Being your Guardian Angel is all I know."

"Will that change now?" Her heart rate increased slightly at the thought of losing his company.

"No. I will always be your Guardian Angel." He gave her arm a squeeze.

"Yeah, but now I'll have to find a bigger dumpster to sleep in."

He yanked her hat from her head, then mussed her hair.

"Hey? What did you do that for?" she said, reaching for the hat he held above her head.

"I've always wanted to do that," he said. Their gazes locked. "You have the prettiest hair I've ever seen."

She lowered her eyes then looked back into his. "Thank you." The few moments of teasing endeared him to her. Her father had teased her when she was growing up and she missed it.

He set her hat down and caught her hands in his, running the pads of his thumbs against her palms. "You are a beautiful young woman. Quit hiding behind these…ugly clothes."

"You know why I do it," she whispered, lowering her eyes once more. Another month of working and she would be able to pay her back rent. Then Mr. Turner would give her the contents of the apartment, but she would still be homeless, unless she could come up with another month's rent.

"I know." Mike slowly pulled his hands away but held her sad gaze.

"Tell me, Mike, what you remember…about your past?" she asked, changing the subject.

"Like I said before, all I remember is being your Guardian Angel. I didn't know that I had a past." He looked up to heaven, then back at her. "But the taste of the coffee and food are familiar to me, as if I had them before."

When Mike had caressed her hands, warmth emanated from her flesh and burned into him, making another memory he wouldn't forget. The feel of her silky hair beneath his fingers, and her soft, smooth skin brought on that strange sensation he had experienced earlier. It was a pleasing sensation that alerted his body in a way that was familiar yet new. And he didn't want the sensations to stop. In fact, he wanted to touch more of her flesh—

"Were you…married?" Her question interrupted his thoughts.

"I…don't remember," he said, searching his mind for anything that could answer that question. A question he never would have entertained had he remained a spirit being.

She looked at him differently now, with an expectancy he had never seen before. His heart rate increased.

Why was he having these flashes of memories while in the flesh and why these new feelings?

"Here's your check," Susan said, turning the paper upside down in front of him.

María took the receipt and looked at it, then pulled her change purse out of her coat pocket. Withdrawing enough funds to cover the two meals plus a tip, she left the money on the table.

"I'll be right back," she said, getting up. She headed for the restroom.

Mike couldn't let her out of his sight, so he turned back into a spirit being.

María returned to the dining room, but Mike was nowhere in sight. Some Guardian Angel he turned out to be.

"Hmmm." He helped her spend her money and then took off. She'd been on a couple of dates that ended that way. Why did she always fall for guys like that? She didn't even see it coming. She stepped out the door and looked up and down the deserted street. The bus wouldn't be running for another hour.

The Greasy Spoon was a couple miles from there. The walk would do her good with all she had to think about.

Having breakfast with an angel was a new experience for her, especially one as good looking as Mike. She shoved her hands in her pockets as a cool, crisp breeze stirred the air. She thought about the cute dimple on Mike's face.

She headed downtown on Ninth Avenue. How many other people had seen their Guardian Angel, she wondered. There was something about him that fascinated her. More questions formed in her head as she walked. She didn't get to ask why he dressed the way he did, or how he transported them across town. Had she imagined the past hour?

Chapter Two

Mike floated beside María as a spirit being. She made him feel things he hadn't felt before. What was happening to him? In all the time he had been her Guardian Angel, he couldn't remember the feelings or sensations he experienced while being in the flesh. Had he really been human? Did he have these feelings then?

As long as he remained a pure spirit being, he had no sense of touch, taste or smell. He knew emotions, but not to the extent he'd felt them briefly tonight. His senses had gone into overdrive.

Something new affected him, though. He glanced at her while she walked. When he caressed her hands earlier, he didn't want to stop. In fact, he *desired* to feel more of her skin beneath his fingers, to hold her face in his hands. He didn't yield to that desire, though. Instead, he infused her with a sense of calm, something she needed.

The sparkle in her eyes, which had been gone since her mother's death, was back tonight. He could feel a passion rising within her.

Then he thought about his recent discoveries. When he tasted and smelled the eggs, it brought back memories. At first, it was glimpses of the past, where he was eating at that particular restaurant while sitting with a man. Could it have been a partner? Then other memories came into focus. More like glimpses of people. The memories were still fuzzy, but the fact that he *had* memories was puzzling.

Then there was the feeling of hunger. The hunger for food, the hunger for adventure, the hunger for…a woman. Did he have someone in his life before this? He couldn't remember. But he remembered the sensations he felt when he held María against his body in the dumpster. It was a different sensation than the one he felt when he held her as they moved through time.

Thinking of the warmth of her body made him desire to hold her once more. He looked heavenward. *Lord, I need your help in this matter.*

Fighting off the spiritual demons that wreaked havoc on humans had been difficult, but to fight off the temptations of the flesh was another battle altogether. He was going to need all the help he could get.

• • •

Taylor Sanders pulled his black, 1998 Buick LeSabre to a stop in front of an alley. Two men stepped out of the shadows and approached his vehicle.

"Everything okay, gentlemen?" Sanders asked, his arm resting on the window of his car.

"A minor setback, otherwise everything went well," Bannen answered.

"Setback?" He didn't like the sound of that.

"Yeah, someone saw the transactions," Coulter added.

"What do you mean, someone saw you?" Sanders demanded, deepening his voice and leaning out the car window. That wasn't good.

"We took care of it," Bannen said, raising his hands, gesturing to hold on.

Sanders scowled and tensed his jaw. He would have to do something about Bannen and Coulter. They made too many mistakes.

"We couldn't let him walk with that information, now could we?" Coulter asked.

Sanders ran his hand through his hair, grinding his teeth once more. He definitely would have to do something about these two men.

"Damnation! I guess not. I can't have that. You two better be more careful in the future." Yeah, he would call Roberts tonight and have *him* deal with them.

Coulter pulled his jacket back and stuffed his hands in his jeans pockets. "We ditched the body under the overpass," he whispered.

Sanders waved a finger at Coulter. "I told you I don't want to hear that kind of information. Keep it to yourself."

Gnashing his teeth together several times, he put the car in drive and floored it. He had to get away from them. Bannen and Coulter had caused him more problems than he anticipated. They were getting sloppy, and he couldn't afford that. He reached for his cell phone and punched in Roberts' number.

"What is it?" Roberts answered.

"Keep an eye on Bannen and Coulter. They're getting sloppy. Too many mistakes and they'll get caught."

"What do you mean?"

"You'll find their latest mistake under the overpass, downtown. I won't be cleaning up their messes."

"Don't forget who you're working for, Sanders," Roberts said, then disconnected.

• • •

María sat down on the concrete entrance to The Greasy Spoon. The step was cold on her bottom as she waited with her knees bent and her arms folded atop, her head resting on her arms.

A man approached her from the side of the building a short time later.

"Good morning, child. What are you doing here so early?"

Mr. Brodsky looked at his watch as he stepped beside her to unlock the door. "Have you been here long?"

"I…uh…couldn't sleep." María shrugged. "I've only been here a few minutes," she lied, as she stood up and followed Mr. Brodsky inside. The sun peeked over the top of the buildings toward the east as she closed the door behind her.

She hung up her father's old jacket and hat, then put on her apron. While Mr. Brodsky readied the kitchen, María put out the silverware, restocked the plates and glassware, and set up the dining room for the morning and lunch crowd. Mrs. Brodsky and her daughter, Diane, arrived later and pitched in. The Greasy Spoon was a family-run diner.

"Um, Mr. Brodsky?" María began.

"Yes, María?"

"Do you think I could leave a little early today?"

"Sure. Is everything all right?"

"I saw something last night, and I need to report it to the police." She held her breath. She couldn't let on that she lived on the streets. That was one secret she kept from them.

"What happened?" he asked, holding his hand over the onions he had been chopping.

She swallowed. How could she tell him without giving herself away?

"A murder," she whispered.

"Murder? You saw a murder?"

"Yes. Promise not to tell anyone, okay?"

"If you are going to the police, why should I keep it a secret?" He set his knife down.

María hesitated. "You don't want them looking for you, now, do you?"

"Are they looking for you?" he asked, wiping his hands on his apron.

"I don't think so but the fewer people who know what I saw, the better."

He nodded. "How early do you want off?"

Hours later, María finished cleaning the dishwashing pit, and hung her apron up shortly after 2 p.m. She quickly showered in the employee bathroom and slipped on clean underwear she kept in a zip-lock bag inside her interior coat pocket. The others she stashed in another baggie. There was plenty of time to see the police about what happened earlier this morning, but first she had to make a deposit. She slipped her father's wrinkled jacket back on and pulled her combed, wet hair up under her hat.

"See you tomorrow, Mr. Brodsky," she said as she left.

After making her weekly deposit, María made her way toward the Police Department off Alcaniz Street. It was close to 4 p.m. by the time she got there. She stood outside the door and took a deep breath, closing her eyes momentarily.

You're not alone. She heard Mike's voice in her head. Turning around, she made sure no one else was there.

It would be easier if you were here in person. She spoke to him through her mind. Had he been there the whole time?

Yes. I'm always here.

María stepped inside and approached the desk. A shiver from her cold, wet hair ran through her body.

"I need to talk to somebody about a murder," she began.

The officer cocked his head. "What did you say?"

She leaned closer. "I saw a murder early this morning, and I'm here to report what I saw," she said nervously, her mouth dry.

"Wait here," he said, pointing at her as he moved away from the counter.

María looked around the office, until a man approached her.

"Can I help you?" the gentleman said, his arms folded across his chest. He wore a light green dress shirt and matching tie with abstract designs on it, along with hunter green dress pants.

"I…uh…I'm here to report a murder," she whispered.

He nodded. "Follow me." He turned and walked through a doorway. The man was about six feet tall. He stopped at an empty desk in a room full of desks, where men and women talked on phones, worked at computers, or spoke with people sitting with them.

"Have a seat," He pointed to the chair next to his workstation as he sat down. "The name's Detective Taylor Sanders," He offered his hand.

María took his hand and shook it. His strong grip squeezed her hand to the point of pain. "María Rojas," she said, squeezing back as hard as she could, but his strength was far greater. *Was this a game he was playing?*

"Last night, a man was murdered near Tarragona Street," she began.

"Wait," He held up his hand. "I need some information from you, like your address." He typed something onto his keyboard.

"Why?"

"For the report." He turned to look at her. "In case I need to contact you later for further questioning."

She closed her eyes. How was she going to get through this?

Tell the truth. Mike said in her head.

She took a deep breath. "Okay."

Sanders immediately typed on his keyboard. "Where do you live, María?"

She gave him the post office box she had when she had been in transition. She seldom checked it anymore, but it was paid for.

"That's a mailing address. I need a street address. Where do you *live?*" he asked.

"I'd rather not give it to you just now," she stalled.

He looked at her, his eyes narrowed.

"Well, then, how about your phone number?" He glared at her.

"Don't have one."

"How do you communicate with people?" He appeared annoyed. His graying hair and eyebrows, along with the wrinkles across his forehead, showed him to be in his late forties, possibly fifties.

"In person mostly."

"What about your parents? How do they get in touch with you?" He gestured with his hands.

"They…" she lowered her head, her eyes watering from the memory. "They are both deceased." She blinked away the tears.

He crossed his arms over his chest, tightening his lips into a frown. "When did you say this murder occurred?"

"This morning, sometime before 4:00."

He began typing again. "And where were *you* when this alleged incident took place?"

"I was…near Tarragona Street," María scratched the side of her head, then folded her hands in her lap. She began twiddling her thumbs, a habit her mother had when she had been nervous.

"What were you doing there at that time of the morning?"

"Ummm…walking. I was…walking home…from a party."

"And where was this party?"

"The party has nothing to do with this."

"Maybe someone there saw the murder."

"No. No one saw the murder but me." She stopped her thumbs.

"How do you know that?"

"Because I was there. No one else saw it. Okay?" She clenched her hands tight.

He typed a few things then turned to face her. "What happened, María? What exactly did you see?"

"An old man, Joe Blue, was…killed by two men. One stuck him with a taser, and the other man injected him with some sort of drug."

"Joe Blue?"

"He's a…was a…homeless man I'd met once. He liked collecting anything that was blue. Whenever I saw him, he pushed a grocery cart full of blue…things."

Sanders stopped typing and turned to look at her.

"What is it you want, María?" He studied her.

María cocked her head. "What do you mean?" She felt uncomfortable.

"You know what I mean. Do you want money for drugs? Is that why you're here? Or are you a prostitute?"

"Excuse me?" María's pulse quickened, while her face grew hot.

"There was no murder on Tarragona this morning, María, and you know it." He stood up facing her, his arms crossed over his chest.

"You know something," she said, standing, her fists clenched at her sides. "You can believe nothing happened if you want, but it's a lie. Joe Blue was murdered this morning, and I saw the whole thing." She turned and headed toward the door, bumping into a tall man in a dark suit.

He touched her shoulder and looked into her eyes. "Excuse me," he said. "Are you all right?"

"No." She pushed past him, feeling a cold chill run up her spine as she thought of Sanders and her conversation. There was something about Sanders that unnerved her.

So much for doing the right thing, she thought, standing on the steps of the Pensacola Police Department. Now she needed a new place to sleep. The old neighborhood was no longer safe.

Sanders looked at his watch. Damnation. That's all he needed now, on top of the mistakes Bannen and Coulter had made.

"Having problems, Sanders?" Detective Anderson asked.

"No. No problems." He closed out the report without saving the changes. "Why do you ask?"

Anderson stood at Sanders' desk, staring at Sanders' computer. "What was the young lady's complaint?"

"She was a hooker looking for money, so I sent her away," he lied. Anderson had always been a pain in his side. He was too damn nosy for his own good.

Anderson nodded, then left. Good. He had to make another call, but not here. Sanders grabbed his suit jacket and left the office.

There was something prickly about that girl, but Sanders couldn't figure out what it was.

• • •

Mike had stayed busy with the two evil spirits that hovered over Sanders. The fire darts were easily deflected with his shield, but their sword work left a lot to be desired. Mike managed to keep them back with the Sword of Truth, eventually tiring the two demons and they fled.

Evil spirits hovering over the other officers in the room joined in the fight initially, but Mike had help from the Guardian Angels who were present.

If only humans could see the battles being fought for their souls, they would protect themselves more, he thought.

For some reason, though, Sanders and the gentleman María bumped into looked familiar to him. He shook off those thoughts as he followed after her.

• • •

María made her way downtown. She was early, but the priest always seemed to welcome her help.

"Hello, Father Bivens, Mr. Ricks," she said as she entered the Soup Kitchen. It had once been an office building, standing vacant for many years. Part of it was converted into a kitchen and dining room used to prepare meals for the homeless. It smelled of new paint.

During the nights, the remaining space was converted into a homeless shelter. She slept there a few times in the beginning, when her world came crashing down on her.

"Are you anticipating a large crowd tonight, Father?" she asked, when she saw the extra helpers in the kitchen.

"The weather is changing, María, so I expect more every night."

María helped set up the rows of tables, then worked in the kitchen pulling bread from the oven for the meal.

People trickled in about 6:00 p.m., and then it grew steady until 7:30 p.m. She served the steaming bowls of vegetable soup, while others helped with silverware, bread and drinks. Her heart was heavy at seeing so many people each night without homes. All of them had their own stories to tell.

Big Tom came in with Doc. She looked over at Father Bivens.

"Go ahead, María, get something to eat before it's all gone."

Taking her bowl of soup, bread and drink, María headed toward the table. Big Tom and Doc had been the only two to befriend her in her grief the first few days on the streets. They had looked after her, giving her tips on how to survive.

"Hey," she said, slipping into the seat, beside the bearded, dark-haired man.

"I seen Joe Blue's grocery cart this morning on Tarragona, but no Joe," Tom said, taking a bite of bread. He wore his long-sleeved, unbuttoned tattered denim shirt over a black T-shirt and jeans. Tom was a robust man, standing over six feet tall. He kept to himself mostly.

María had just taken a sip of her soup and choked at his words.

Tom patted her back. "You okay?"

She hung her head low over her bowl. What could she say? How could she tell him?

"You know something, don't you?" Doc asked. He was wearing his old brown pullover sweater and khaki pants.

She glanced up at him and nodded.

"I heard they found a body under the overpass," Doc continued. Gray stubble had grown on his face since the last time she had seen him.

"When?" Tom asked.

"This morning."

Tom put his hand on her back. She forced the soup down.

"Who was it?" Tom asked.

She glanced up at him. "I saw Joe Blue this morning," she began. Looking down, she stirred her soup. "Two men…killed him…because he saw something. They hauled his body off." Mike's words came back to her from this morning. "That was Joe under the overpass."

Tom slammed his beefy fist down on the table, startling everyone. "Joe never hurt anybody." He stood up and headed for the door.

María turned to watch him leave. "Should I go after him, Doc?"

"Leave him be. Joe got him off alcohol a year ago, and they had been friends since then."

She tensed her jaw, remembering Joe's final words, 'I don't want any trouble.'

María lost her appetite but waited for Doc to finish his meal. "I reported the murder to the police, Doc, but they didn't believe me."

Doc shook his head. "To them, the homeless don't mean a thing."

"I'm looking for a new place to sleep, Doc," María said, once they were outside.

"What about here?" he suggested, referring to the Homeless Shelter.

"No…I'd rather have my own place."

"I hear you. But your old place is definitely not safe."

"The plaza looks good," she said, as she walked beside Doc.

"The cops patrol it."

Not good. They would only make her leave to find another place.

Just past the park, María spied a couple of men standing around a trash can on the sidewalk, with a fire burning inside. The two were warming their hands. The cool air was brisk, and the night promised to get colder.

María and Doc stopped and joined the strangers, exchanging pleasantries.

The thought of one day having her own home with a fireplace and a husband, helped warm her. Closing her eyes briefly, she envisioned the brown-eyed man with dark hair and a dimple on his left cheek smiling at her.

I could get used to having him around, she thought. Her cheeks heated from imagining him standing behind her with his arms wrapped around her waist, his cheek next to hers and whispering something sexy in her ear.

"I guess I'll see you tomorrow, Doc," she said as she slowly turned to leave.

"Take care," he called after her.

She shoved her hands in her pockets and headed towards the plaza. There were trees there that she would climb to stay hidden from the cops. She would wake early enough to avoid being seen.

As she walked toward an alley, she thought of all those people who ate at the Soup Kitchen. Just because they were homeless didn't mean they didn't have the same basic needs as everyone else. Life just hit them hard at the worst possible moment. No one wanted to be homeless. It just…happened.

Doc had been a college professor with a doctorate degree. One day, he came home from work to find his wife in bed with the Dean of Academic Affairs. His wife took everything he owned. After the divorce, he lost his job due to cuts in the budget. He found himself completely alone and homeless with no income. So, Doc traded employment for lodging at a hotel by doing maintenance work.

María stepped out onto a nearby street. If only she was as lucky as Doc. The Brodsky family had been nice to her, and she got a free afternoon meal and daily shower, but what little money she earned working there was going to pay off her debt to Mr. Turner so she could get her belongings back. That is, if he still had them.

The sound of car tires rolling slowly over asphalt brought her thoughts to a halt. She glanced over her shoulder.

A white car moved slowly down the center of the street toward her. Her pulse quickened. There were no lights on that car. She glanced around for an escape. The plaza was a block away.

The car sped up. She took off. Legs pumped. Heart pounded. At the corner, the car bore down on her.

Suddenly, someone shoved her away from the car, rolling with her on the ground, cushioning her fall. Tires screeched to a halt. The smell of burning rubber filled the air. In the distance, she heard sirens. When she lifted her head up off the ground, she saw the car speeding away with the sirens getting louder and closer.

CHAPTER THREE

"Are you all right?" Mike asked, helping María to her feet.

María nodded. "What just happened?" She noticed the sirens had stopped. Touching her head, she discovered her hat was missing.

"Someone tried to kill you," he said, bending over to retrieve her hat from under a bush. He was still dressed in the strange garb she had seen before, and his taut, muscular thighs drew her full attention.

Shaking the thoughts from her head, María glanced around the plaza and made sure the car was gone. "Where are the cops when you need them?"

"That was me making the siren sound," Mike said, approaching her.

"Really? What else can you do?"

"I can move objects, take on different forms, or no form at all, I can change things, or comfort you. As a Guardian Angel, I battle evil spirits to protect you."

María realized that the short, skirt-like outfit, coupled with the shiny silver breastplate that Mike wore over his bare chest, had been a uniform of sorts. "So that's why you dress like that?" She cocked her head.

"These garments are the armor of God, my battle dress, you might say."

María noticed a sword sheathed at his side, and silver bands covering his forearms. *Had those been there before?*

"No, to answer your question. When we met in the dumpster, the sword and arm bands weren't needed."

"Why now?" María asked.

"You've picked up a few enemies since your report to the police. The car that tried to run you down was surrounded by evil spirits. I fought them until the driver sped up, then my priorities changed immediately."

"Will he be back?"

"Not tonight. He thinks he hit you, so he's satisfied for now."

"Why would he think that?" She scratched her temple.

"Because I dented his car to make him believe he hit you. He will report the incident to his boss. It'll be awhile before he realizes his mistake."

"What makes you so sure?"

"I told you, I know a lot of things. Angels have more knowledge than humans. We know things that you cannot know. If you had trusted me more, María, you wouldn't be in this mess in the first place."

"Why should I trust you? You left me alone in that restaurant."

"You weren't alone. I couldn't let you out of my sight."

"You…mean you were in the bathroom with me?"

"No. Once I knew you were alone inside, I stood guard outside. I do respect your privacy, María, unless your safety is jeopardized."

She lowered her head, then shook it. "I've got to find a new place to sleep tonight." She raised her head and felt drawn into Mike's eyes. "I have to be awake early for my job at the Greasy Spoon."

He pulled her close and plopped her hat on her head. "I know just the place," he said, wrapping his arms around her. In the next instant, they were at Seville Square.

"How…exactly…did you do that?" María looked up at him, amazed, her arms still around him.

He half smiled when he glanced at her. "I just thought myself here." He winked.

She smiled as she slowly pulled away from him and walked toward a bench. Looking at him made her feel good. She hugged her arms in the cool breeze and thought of that sexy smile.

"I guess this will have to do," she said, sitting down and shaking the thought of his full lips from her mind.

Mike sat next to her. "Lay your head on my lap and sleep."

"Aren't you tired?"

"Angels don't sleep. I'll watch over you tonight, like I always do."

"But don't the cops patrol this area?"

"They won't see you. I'll make sure of that."

María curled up next to him on the bench, resting her head on his bare, muscular thigh. She shivered as she made the sign of the cross and quickly mumbled her prayer.

"Cold?" he asked.

"Yes."

Mike waved his hand in the air and suddenly, warmth flowed around her. She settled against him as he ran a hand through her hair, his other hand rested against her shoulder. His gentle touch lulled her to sleep in minutes.

Mike set María's hat to the side and ran his fingers through her hair, combing it away from her face. The softness of her tresses seemed to soothe his restlessness. He watched her relax and finally drift off to sleep. She had a hard life. He wished he could tell her how to fix things, but he wasn't allowed to interfere with free will. He could guide her, but she had to choose to listen.

The temptation to remain human was strong. How would he explain himself to those who knew her? Would she like him tagging along everywhere? He glanced down at her sleeping frame and smiled. Her thoughts of him gave her away. She enjoyed his company as much as he enjoyed hers.

The more he caressed her head, the more he wanted to touch her face and trace her features with his fingers. From the moment she was born, he had been drawn to that beautiful face.

He waited hours until she was sound asleep and allowed the back of his fingers to lightly graze her cheeks. Then, using the pads of his fingers, he stroked her face.

The softness of her skin felt velvety to his touch. The smile on her face sent a strange sensation to his stomach, like nervous excitement. The memory of a blonde woman lying in his arms flashed through his mind. He sat up and tried to replay the image, but it wouldn't come. Who *was* that?

Daylight would be upon them in a few hours. While María worked, he would become invisible so others wouldn't see him. It would be awkward for her to explain his presence to her boss. But she *did* like his company, so he would return for her sake at night, when she was loneliest.

María needed a man in her life, someone to love her the way she deserved.

• • •

Blocks away, at the Ninth Avenue Waffle House, Susan poured Detective Taylor Sanders a cup of coffee.

"Haven't seen you here in a while, Detective. How've you been?" Susan asked.

"Good," he lied, as he looked around the place. He felt uneasy. Hopefully, Roberts took care of the problem with Bannen and Coulter and tied up the loose ends with the girl.

"What can I get you tonight?" Susan's hand poised over her order pad.

"Nothing right now. I'm waiting for someone." He hoped she would take the hint and leave him alone.

"Suit yourself, detective." She turned to leave but hesitated then turned back.

Now what?

"You know, Detective," she began. "I saw a man in here the other day who looked just like your old partner." She stood there with one hand on her hip, the other still clutching her pad and pen.

He hadn't had a partner since Ryan's death twenty-three years earlier. "That's impossible. My partner was killed by drug dealers years ago. It was in all the papers, don't you remember?"

"Yes, I remember," she nodded, and returned to the kitchen.

How ironic. The nightmare that woke him forty-five minutes ago was all about Ryan's death. He hadn't been able to sleep, so he came here. This was where he and Ryan had breakfast at least once a week for four years, while on the graveyard shift.

He looked at his watch. Where was Roberts, anyway? His cell phone rang.

"Sanders here," he said.

"I thought you took care of the police?" Roberts said.

"What do you mean?"

"I hit the girl, but I heard a siren the moment she was down, so I couldn't check for a pulse."

"Are you sure you hit her?"

"Positive. She put a big dent in my fender, and that's coming out of your take." Click. Roberts was gone.

He didn't get to ask about Bannen and Coulter, or the next drop. Well, Roberts would call again. He always did.

Sanders threw some money on the table and left. He would have to see about filling his old prescription for sleeping pills. Scratching his head, he wondered what had caused those old nightmares to return. He shoved his hands into his sweater pockets. He hadn't thought of Ryan since the funeral. And he learned that Susan had seen someone who looked like Ryan, just when Sanders had the irresistible urge to return here after such a long time. How odd.

• • •

"Wake up," a deep, soothing male voice whispered in María's ear.

She was on her side, her head on a firm pillow. When she stretched her arms and legs, her eyes flew open. The pillow was a man's bare leg! María jumped off the bench. Twisting around to see who was there, she stumbled and fell.

Mike laughed at her as she sat on the dew-laden grass.

"You're still here." She smiled with relief.

"I told you, María, I'm always here, whether you see me or not."

He looked good in the morning, and he was still wearing his battle regalia. "How about we get you some clothes today at the Goodwill?" she suggested.

"I have clothes."

"People will wonder about you if they see you dressed like that."

"Let them wonder."

"And if they ask, what will you tell them?"

"Just what I told you." He grinned as he stood and stretched his limbs.

"Yeah, and the cops will haul your butt to jail."

"You let me worry about that," Mike replied.

"Sure, whatever you say." She bent at the waist to twist her hair up under her hat. When she straightened, she lost her balance. Mike was there instantly to catch her, his arms around her waist, as he stood behind her.

"How did you move so fast? You were on the bench—"

"Speed of thought," he whispered in her ear. The sound of his deep, sexy voice and the feel of his warm breath against her skin sent shivers throughout her body. The sweet déjà vu memory of this very moment, last night, came back to her.

She closed her eyes momentarily, savoring the warm touch of his arms around her, and a sweet, cinnamon scent at the closeness of his body.

He cuddled her against his chest. "We could eat at the Waffle House again," he suggested.

She ran her fingers against the dark curly hair on his forearms. If only she could wake up like this every morning.

The next instant, she was standing in front of the Waffle House on Ninth Avenue.

Mike held the door for her as she stepped inside and headed for the ladies' room. She liked his manners, though she wasn't used to men holding doors for her.

When she finished in the ladies' room, she found Mike dressed in blue jeans, white running shoes, and a blue and white plaid, button down shirt, with the tails out.

"You look good in those clothes. Where did you get them?" she asked as she followed him to the booth.

"I thought them on." Mike sat across from her.

The same waitress they'd had the other night approached the table. She set a couple of mugs down and poured coffee for both of them. "Same as the last time, folks?" she asked.

"Sure, but how do you remember us?" María asked. She looked at the creamer Susan placed in front of her.

"I remember a lot of things. I may have trouble with names, but I do remember details," she said, glancing at Mike. "Like your old partner. He was here over an hour ago." She put her hand on her hip, as though she was waiting for his response.

"You must have me mixed up with someone else," Mike said.

"Do I? I did some research after your last visit." She pulled a folded piece of paper out of her apron pocket and set it on the table. "Go ahead and read it," she instructed.

Mike unfolded the paper. It looked like a photocopy of a newspaper article. María moved beside Mike to read with him. There was an image of Mike in the article, wearing a police uniform and hat. He was handsome, but the article was sobering. The headline read: TWO KILLED IN DRUG BUST.

The article continued. Officer Mike Ryan, a five-year veteran of the Pensacola Police Department, was killed Friday night during a drug bust. His partner, Officer Taylor Sanders, was able to kill the perpetrator when the exchange of gun fire led to the death of Ryan. Officer Ryan leaves behind a wife and an infant son.

Mike's mouth dropped open as he stared at the paper in his hand. María placed her hand on his back. "Mike, I'm sorry."

Susan sat down opposite María and Mike. "Tell me Mr. Ryan, who exactly are you?"

Mike looked at María, then Susan. "Where did you get this article?" Mike asked.

"At the library. They have newspaper articles in their database," Susan explained.

"You may be able to find your family and remember your past," María suggested.

"Do you have amnesia or something?" Susan asked.

"Or something." Mike said.

Susan cocked her head. "Mike Ryan died over twenty-three years ago. When he was alive, I served him and his partner when they came to eat here in the early mornings on graveyard shift. *Who* are *you?*"

Mike glanced at María and then back at Susan. "I'm María's Guardian Angel, Susan. I have been for twenty-two years now. And until this moment, I had no memory of ever being human."

"Angels don't lie," María added.

Susan stared at him, her mouth open and eyes large.

Memories of people flashed through Mike's mind rapidly. The blonde woman he had once held in his arms had been Leah, his wife. He had a memory of arriving home, dressed in a police uniform, his hat under his arm. Leah had greeted him at the door with a passionate kiss and a warm embrace. With the memories came a flood of emotions. What was happening to him?

He dropped the article on the table and touched Susan's arm. He could sense her rapid pulse rate and the confusion running through her mind. He infused her with peace.

"May I keep this article, Susan?" He looked through her eyes and into her heart.

"Yes, of course," she nodded. "You know, I really missed seeing you here. I'm sorry about…what happened."

Mike forced a smile. "Thanks. I have a lot to think about right now. Could we have the special again?"

"Sure." Susan patted his arm and left.

He turned to face María. "Since I initially manifested in the flesh, I'd only had a few flashes of memories that I didn't understand, María. But since I've read this article," he tapped the paper with his finger, "the memories are becoming clearer now."

"Like what?" María asked.

"My wife's name is Leah, but I don't remember having a child. I remember being in uniform once and coming home. Some memories are merely glimpses of people, places, or things."

"What kind of things?" she asked.

"Objects. Some are just blurs." He closed his eyes momentarily, trying to focus on anything, but nothing would come.

Susan set their plates of eggs, hash browns, sausage and toast in front of them. María attacked her food.

Mike shook his head and smiled. She must be hungry. He couldn't remember her eating with such gusto in a long time.

She looked up at him, her mouth full, and smiled.

While he ate, Mike's thoughts darted in different directions. Some images played in his mind of eating at the Waffle House, only different meals with male laughter in the background. Then there were whispered conversations with another male, only his face was blurred. There were glimpses of a celebration in a…church hall. He was dressed in a tuxedo, and there was a beautiful blonde woman in white…Leah. Their wedding. Faces faded into the background as the two of them danced. Then, there was an older woman with graying hair, smiling at him—his mother. A man came up beside her—his dad.

"Mike," María tugged on his arm. He looked over at her.

"You were staring into space. What's wrong?"

"I…had some memory flashes…of being here before."

"And…your wife?"

He nodded. "I remember feelings as well."

María's hand paused over her toast. "Why don't you stay in the flesh? Maybe your memory will return faster."

Mike placed his hand on her shoulder, hugging her. "And what will I do all day?"

"I'll talk to Mr. Brodsky. They've been busy at the Greasy Spoon lately. I could help his daughter as a server, and you could do the dishes." She wiggled a brow at him.

He knew she didn't like doing the dishes, but it was the only job she could get at the time. He smiled at her. There was so much about María that he liked, and now he

felt tenderness toward her that he had never felt before. She was actually trying to help him. *We'll have to do something about your clothes, then, won't we?* He spoke to her mind. He sensed the electricity between them. How long had that been present without him knowing?

She smiled up at him. He liked her smile, though lately, she didn't have much to be happy about.

After breakfast, Mike remained in the flesh, walking beside María to the Greasy Spoon. The sights looked familiar. The sounds and smells of the pre-dawn brought more memories of driving through the neighborhood in a patrol car early in the morning.

It was still dark when he and María arrived at the Greasy Spoon. He pulled her to a stop. "We need to make you look like server material."

"How do we do that?"

"Take off your hat." He held his hand out to her. "Brush."

She handed him the brush from her inside coat pocket. He brushed her long, brown hair back from her face. The thick mass was soft and silky in his hands as he braided her tresses. He had longed to touch her hair while he was an angel, to experience what softness felt like against his flesh.

An image of their naked bodies entwined in a passionate kiss played across his mind. His body reacted instantly with a surge of heat blossoming into strong desire.

"That felt so good," María whispered, bringing him out of his thoughts. What was happening to him? He had never had thoughts of her like that before. But he'd never had feelings like these before either, at least not since he had been an angel.

At the end of María's brush was an elastic band he used to contain the thick mass of hair.

He stepped away from her as she turned around. The new feelings he experienced were vivid and strong, as if the feelings had been trapped inside him for a long time and now pushed to escape.

"Diane wears a black dress with a white apron when she serves," María began.

"Yes, and Mr. Brodsky has an extra one in his office for when Mrs. Brodsky helps out."

"How do you know…uh, never mind," she said, frowning.

He smiled at her and lifted her chin. "Mr. Brodsky is here. You won't see me until he agrees to hire me." He evaporated from her sight and watched her look around.

"Good morning, María," Mr. Brodsky said to her. "Ah, you've done something to your hair. It looks good."

"Thank you. Umm, Mr. Brodsky?"

"Yes?" He unlocked the door.

"I was wondering if I could start serving here."

"Well, Diane does need some help in the mornings. But what would I do about the dishes?"

"I know the perfect person for the job," she said, following him in the door.

Mike watched her convince Mr. Brodsky to hire him. He was amazed at her determination, a behavior he had seen before when she had studied nursing.

"Okay, okay," Mr. Brodsky raised his hands in defeat.

"I'll go get him," María said, darting out the back door.

He manifested instantly before her. "Good job," he said, palms up. She slapped his palms.

"Come on, then," she tugged at his arm. "I'll show you the routine."

Her touch sent a warm shiver through his body. He remembered that sensation from before, but had he felt that way when Leah touched him?

María showed him the routine with the Hobart equipment, explaining how important it was to do things properly.

"María, I'm good," Mike touched her shoulder and looked deeply into her eyes. Had she forgotten he had seen her do this for a couple months now?

She looked puzzled at his remark.

"I know what to do here, remember? I've seen you wash dishes every day."

María rolled her eyes and hit her forehead with the palm of her hand. She had been working here several months now. What had she been thinking? He saw everything she did. He knew her most intimate thoughts. Her cheeks grew hot at the thought of him knowing what she had been thinking earlier when he had brushed her hair. *Lord help me.*

Mrs. Brodsky's outfit was a little large, but with the belted waist, she was able to take up some of the slack. She hung her father's clothes up in the employee bathroom and stepped out the door, bumping into Mike.

"Nice," he said, grinning and giving her the once over.

Her cheeks burned at his gaze and she turned away. Mike grabbed her arm, and she turned back to face him.

Hot!

"What?" she asked softly, meeting his intense gaze. Did she just hear his thoughts?

"Uh…good luck, María," he said, releasing her arm.

María watched Mike head for the Hobart before turning away. Maybe she misunderstood what he had said. Did angels actually think like that? A large grin grew across her face.

Diane went over a few tips on serving the guests, taking orders that Mr. Brodsky could understand, and pre-busing the tables.

When the guests trickled in, the pace was steady. She and Diane took turns. She had no trouble with the menu, since she had eaten here every day, but the trays of food were heavy.

One guest, however, stood out. He looked familiar, but she couldn't place where she'd seen him. He made her feel uneasy, as she poured him a cup of coffee.

"Have you decided what you want, sir?" she asked as politely as she could, taking out her pad and pen.

"Eggs over medium, sausage patties with biscuits instead of toast. And I want grits." He eyed her suspiciously.

When she brought his plate of food, she also carried the pot of coffee for a refill. Setting the plate before him, she poured the coffee as he spoke.

"What can you tell me about the murder of that homeless man found under the overpass?"

Her hand jerked at the mention of murder, and the coffee spilled over the table.

"Sorry," she said, grabbing napkins and dabbing up the hot liquid. "I'm really sorry. You startled me."

"You know something, don't you?"

"Who…are you?" she squeaked out.

"Detective Anderson of the Pensacola Police Department." He pulled out his badge and flipped it open. She examined it, looking at the image, then the man himself. It looked genuine.

"I reported what I saw to Detective Sanders, but he didn't believe me."

"Suppose you tell me what you saw, and forget what Sanders said."

She squatted down beside him and spoke in a soft tone.

"Joe Blue was chased down an alley the other night off Tarragona Street. Two guys threatened him. One stuck him with a taser. The other stuck him in the arm with a hypodermic needle. When he slumped over, the two men took his body and left."

He leaned towards her. "You saw this?"

"Yes."

"Do you remember what was said?"

"Joe said he didn't want any trouble. One of the men said it was too late because Joe had seen too much already."

"Did they say where they were taking him?"

María hesitated. She knew what Mike had told her but didn't know if she should tell this man. She looked around, to make sure she wasn't needed, then whispered, "Under the overpass." María got up and headed back to the kitchen with the coffee pot, her hands shaking.

She didn't actually lie to him, but that was what Mike had told her, and she believed Mike. Angels didn't lie, since they worked for God.

After checking on her other guests, she stopped by Detective Anderson's table again. "Can I interest you in a piece of apple pie, Detective Anderson?" she asked him.

He handed her his business card. "If you see or hear anything, call me."

She bit her bottom lip. "Someone tried to kill me last night," she whispered.

CHAPTER FOUR

aylor Sanders arrived at the police station early that afternoon. Too early, he thought. Now that the girl was out of the way, he had to make sure there was nothing to tie him to her death.

What was he thinking? Of course, there was nothing. She was hit by a car downtown, and he was having breakfast at the Waffle House, miles away. The old waitress was his alibi. He had a conversation with her, and she remembered him from years ago, when he and Ryan had been partners.

Sanders pulled his chair out from his desk when he saw Anderson lead some people into the interrogation room down the hall. He blinked twice and his heart beat faster when he recognized the girl. She was supposed to be dead! But wait, the guy with her looked like…Mike Ryan? Sanders dropped into his chair, light-headed. His mouth went dry as he ran a hand through his hair. Ryan, no, the man who looked like Ryan, was the same age when Ryan died. Had he imagined that, or did he see two ghosts?

• • •

María arrived at the Pensacola Police Department that afternoon with Mike. She felt more confident with him beside her.

"I hope you don't mind, Detective Anderson, but I brought a friend with me," she said, gesturing to Mike.

Mike reached out his hand to Anderson. "The name's Mike," he said.

Anderson's eyes got large. "Mike Ryan?"

"Uh, Angel. Mike Angel. I was named after Ryan," Mike said.

"You…you look just like him."

Mike nodded.

"Ryan was a good man. All of us were shocked when we learned of his death," Anderson said. "How did you come to be named after him?"

"A relative, you might say," Mike offered.

María glanced at Mike and raised an eyebrow. *Now who was lying?*

Mike tensed his jaw.

"Unfortunately, the killing of the drug dealer hasn't halted the drug traffic all these years. It's more like a plague now," Anderson added.

He ushered them into a room with a long table in the center, with several books on it.

"I want you to look at these mug shots, María," Detective Anderson said, motioning them to sit. "Go through the books and see if anyone looks familiar." Walking back to the door, Anderson hesitated. "Would you two like something to drink?"

"A Coke would be nice," she said.

"Make that two Cokes," Mike added.

"I'll be right back." Anderson left the room.

"Well, Anderson, I see you've got company today," Sanders began. He had to find out what Anderson knew.

Anderson stopped in his tracks. "Yes, someone you know, actually."

Sanders swallowed. "Oh?"

"María Rojas. You remember her, don't you? She's the eye witness to the murder I'm investigating."

"Murder? I thought you were investigating a drug overdose," Sanders said.

"It looked like that initially, but I'm having some things double checked, and I'm following up on a couple leads."

"Who's with her?" Sanders felt a cold sweat break out across his forehead.

Anderson smirked. "You won't believe it, but the guy with her looks just like Mike Ryan."

"Ryan?" Sander's conversation with Susan, the waitress, came to mind, as he moved toward the interrogation room. Looking through the glass in the door, Sanders saw the man standing behind María, glancing over her shoulder. Then, in one swift movement, the man turned his gaze toward Sanders.

Sanders backed away from the door, his heart pounding. He wiped his forehead and hurried out the building.

Carefully, María glanced at each image in the first book, but she didn't recognize any lof them. "I only saw them from the side," she said to Mike. "Did you get a look at them?"

"I was too busy holding you still," he half smiled at her.

She rolled her eyes, as Anderson returned with the drinks.

"Any luck?" Anderson asked, setting a drink in front of each of them.

"I'm sorry, detective, but none of them look familiar in this book."

"Try the other books," Anderson indicated with a head movement. "You know, the autopsy showed Joe Blue overdosed on heroine," he said.

"That's because the creeps injected him with the drug. Joe wouldn't do that." María tightened her fists.

"How do you know?"

"Because he preached against drugs and alcohol. Joe had been an alcoholic." María took a large swallow of her drink. "Did you find Joe's cart?"

"What cart?" Anderson asked.

"Joe never went anywhere without his grocery cart. It was always full of blue things that he collected."

"I'll look into that," Anderson said.

Anderson studied Mike. "The resemblance between you and Ryan is uncanny," he said. "I have an old photo of the two of us fishing, and you look like he did when he was your age."

"I get that a lot," Mike said, looking away from Anderson.

"Well, I'll let you get back to the images and I'll return shortly," Anderson said, leaving.

María continued looking through the digest of photos, while Mike paced the floor. She thought about the lies she and Mike had told recently. Did angels get in trouble for lying?

Mike stopped pacing and glanced at her. She caught his gaze. "I prefer to call it deferring the truth," Mike said. "But lying is not good for anyone. It only gets you into more trouble later on." He approached her at the table and started massaging her shoulders. "Besides, we don't know the full truth about my past…at least, not yet."

María leaned her head back at Mike's touch. "That feels…wonderful," she said. The tension drained from her body while his hands kneaded her neck and shoulder muscles. Mike kissed the top of her head. *What other talents did the man possess?*

I'll be glad to show you…anytime, anyplace.

María's face grew hot. Why did she keep forgetting her thoughts were not private anymore?

Anderson walked into the room. Mike stood behind María, his hands still on her shoulders.

"Any luck?" Anderson asked.

"I'm afraid not," she said, closing the last book.

"Well, I appreciate you coming down here, María," Anderson said.

"It turned out to be a waste of time." She crossed her arms over her chest.

"I wouldn't say that. Maybe looking at these images will jog your memory later," Anderson said, showing them to the door.

"I hope so." María reached the doorway.

"Call me if you remember anything," Anderson added.

Tell him about the shoes, Mike spoke to her mind.

She turned to look at Mike. "Shoes?"

"What about shoes?" Anderson asked, looking at both of them.

"Uh, one of the men had on a pair of white running shoes with a silver lightning bolt design on the side. It sort of glowed when the light hit it," she explained. The little detail had slipped her mind until Mike mentioned it.

Anderson pulled out a pad and pen and jotted something down. "That may be helpful, María. I'll follow up on that. Thanks again." Anderson left.

"Well, did you recognize anybody at all?" María asked Mike when they were on the steps outside the police department. She bent over and twisted her hair, tucking it under her hat.

"I didn't give it my full attention," he said.

"What did you do while I looked through those books?" María tugged her hat back into place.

• • •

Sanders sat in his car and dialed Roberts' number. "I thought you took care of the girl," Sanders whispered harshly.

"I did," Roberts replied.

"Then why was she at the police department a few minutes ago?"

"What are you talking about?"

"You didn't get rid of the body because there was no body," Sanders continued.

"I told you what happened. Maybe she didn't die, but I hit her. I know I did. I have a dented fender to prove it."

"Well, you need to take care of her tonight, once and for all. Another detective has taken an interest in her story."

"Yeah, well you keep the heat off my boys, and I'll deal with the girl," Roberts said.

• • •

Mike ran a hand through his hair. "I remembered things, while you looked at photos, like when I worked at the station.

I remembered Anderson and the fishing trip. We actually fished together a lot. He has a family now, but both of us started out single then got married after we joined the department." He walked beside María toward the Soup Kitchen. "I believe he was more of a friend than my partner, Taylor Sanders."

"What else did you do?"

"I kept away evil spirits."

"Dressed like that? Come on. You should have been wearing your battle armor." She knocked his side with her elbow.

He glanced at her and caught her smile. But when he heard her thoughts, he smiled, and she blushed. "You like my body in that suit, huh?"

"Can't I have one private thought all to myself?" She gestured.

"I like the way your mind works. Listening to your thoughts is very entertaining at times." Lately, though, her thoughts had been more provocative, and it was getting harder to ignore her needs. But as a human, he discovered he had needs of his own, needs that an angel shouldn't even consider.

"Well, I'm glad one of us is entertaining," she said, bringing him out of his thoughts.

A block away from the Soup Kitchen, Mike stopped walking.

"Don't tell me you're leaving me again," she said.

He lifted her chin. He felt her disappointment and saw it in her eyes. She was getting too attached to him, and he couldn't allow that to happen. "It'll be better this way. There are too many evil spirits lurking around some of

the homeless. I have some battles to fight on your behalf to keep me busy, but I'll be with you."

"Yeah, yeah," she said, looking down.

Mike winked out and remained beside her, dressed in his battle uniform once more. He wanted to hold María again, but that was something he would have to get over.

For every Guardian Angel that was out there, an evil spirit lurked nearby, waiting for an opportunity to pounce. Unfortunately, some of the people eating at the Soup Kitchen had more than their share of demons to contend with.

Mike rose and circled María as she walked, deflecting the fiery darts the spirits hurled at her with his shield. Off in the distance, a man he once knew followed María on foot.

At the entrance to the Soup Kitchen, Mike fought a small contingency of Satan's evil cohorts, using the sword of truth to inflict searing pain to each of them, buying María some time.

He remained in position, ready for battle, while María helped the priest with some chores.

• • •

"Good evening, Father Bivens," María said as she walked into the Soup Kitchen.

"Just in time, María. We need help with the chairs," the priest replied.

María set to work opening the chairs while others assisted in situating the chairs around the tables.

Later, she served tea to people in line, wondering when she would see Mike again. She looked forward to his company. Whenever he was around, she felt as if she could handle anything. She hated when he disappeared because that feeling of loneliness crept back, unwelcome. She had to stop thinking about him as part of her life, though. He was just her imagination. Did anyone else have a Guardian Angel half as good looking as hers? Probably not.

Big Tom approached her with his cup. "Hey," she said, dipping the ladle into the container of sweet tea. She looked up at his large frame. His eyes wide, he looked anxious. "What is it, Tom?" she asked.

"I know what Joe saw the other night," Tom whispered.

María spilled some tea while dipping the ladle once more.

"Meet me in the alley off Tarragona tonight around 10 pm," he whispered.

A sinking feeling hit her in the gut. *Don't go.* Was that Mike? She reached for the next person's cup as Tom moved away. Her hands trembled. She wanted to know what Joe saw, but she was afraid. Why couldn't Tom just tell her what he had seen?

When María's replacement showed up, she took her bowl of stew and cup of tea to sit next to Tom. But she didn't see Tom, she saw Doc instead.

"Where's Big Tom?" she asked.

"He left, mumbling something about Joe Blue and the cops," Doc said.

María ate her meal slowly as she thought about Tom's words. What was it that caused those men to kill Joe Blue?

"I saw one of my old colleagues from the junior college at the hotel I'm working at," Doc began.

"Is that good or bad?" María asked.

"Well, he said they may be losing a few professors to retirement next semester." Doc stirred his stew.

"I'll pray for you, Doc," she blurted out. She knew he wanted to go back to teaching. That had been his calling and that's all he ever talked about.

Doc leaned his elbows on the table and looked at her. "After the divorce and losing my job at the college, I never thought I'd get a second chance, María. But I have a good feeling about this," he said, smiling.

María smiled back and offered up a silent prayer. When she finished her stew, Doc walked her out to the park.

"Where are you staying tonight, María?" he asked as they approached a bench.

She glanced down the road. Too many cars moved around, and Tarragona was a block away. The area was busy for a Friday night. "I hadn't thought much about it until now." She remembered the safe feeling she had lying in Mike's arms the night before. If only he was here now. She wanted that feeling of being safe all the time.

"Seville Square would be safer than this place on Friday night," Doc said.

"Yeah, you're right, Doc." She had several blocks to go to get to Seville Square, but she needed to meet Tom first.

Doc walked her partway then headed toward his hotel. María gave him a few minutes, then headed back toward Tarragona.

On her way, she heard Mike's voice. *Don't go. Stay away from there.*

I'll only be a few minutes, she said to Mike in her mind, as she continued down the sidewalk. The evening was cool and crisp as María got closer to her destination.

Tom must have had a good reason for not telling what Joe had seen, but she couldn't figure it out.

As she approached the alley, she heard some scuffling. Her heart skipped a beat. Was that a rat? She hated rats. She stopped at the edge of the building and peered around it.

There was Tom, slumped over a pile of cardboard boxes. Two men stood over his body. One had the same shoes she had described to Anderson earlier. She gasped. The largest man looked right at her. *Oh, God!*

Chapter Five

María turned and ran. Before she reached the end of the block, she was tackled from behind. She fell hard on the concrete sidewalk, but she caught herself with her forearms.

Strong arms pulled at her coat, trying to turn her over. She kicked out with her legs. If she could roll out to the side, maybe she could get away. She propped herself up with her hands, turning her hip to the side, but she was punched hard in the face. "Jesus, help me!" she cried out.

Suddenly, her tormentor was off her. She rolled over and sprang to her feet. Two men struggled in the darkness. The sound of a bone snapping stopped the struggle, but a loud wail came from one of the men. Mike stood up, effortlessly, while the other man half crawled to his feet. One arm hung at a grotesque angle as he fled the area.

María fell into Mike's arms and he held her tight. Her face was numb on one side, and her knees, elbows and hands burned from the abrasions she received in her fall. She should have listened to him. She had heard his voice loud and clear.

"Yes, you should have listened," he whispered as he kissed the top of her head, his arms squeezing her tighter against his chest.

María closed her eyes. Being held in Mike's arms made her feel safe. She tightened her grip around his waist, feeling the pounding of his heart. Silently, they remained locked in each other's embrace a few moments before Mike broke the spell.

He bent to look at her. "You know I can't interfere with free will, María. I called out to you. I know you heard me." His face was full of worry. She reached up and touched his cheek. Caressing Mike's face with her fingers, she gazed at his lips.

"Is Tom dead?" She asked.

"Yes."

"You knew this was going to happen, didn't you?" She looked up into his eyes. Mike nodded.

She closed her eyes, her arms tight around Mike's waist. She would miss Tom. He and Doc were the only two people to befriend her when she was kicked out of her apartment after her mother died of pneumonia. They helped her get through the first month of living on the streets, showing her where to sleep and how to get food. They even introduced her to Mr. Brodsky.

She was safe now. She felt Mike's embrace tighten as heat surged through her body. She glanced up into his eyes as Mike lowered his head, his lips covering her mouth.

The moment his kiss touched her, she felt a jolt of energy shoot through her body, sending a tingling to every nerve ending. Passion burned within her and she wanted Mike. From the way his tongue moved in her mouth, she could tell the feeling was mutual.

Gently pulling away to catch her breath, María realized she was no longer on the ground, but hovering over sand.

"I got a little carried away," he said, half smiling. In an instant, they were standing on the beach.

Mike's lips were moist and swollen from their recent exchange. María let her thumb run across his bottom lip, before she moved closer. When her lips touched his for a second time, a fire ignited in her core. But when she felt the evidence of his arousal, Mike was gone in an instant. María slumped to the sand.

"I'm sorry. I'm sorry. I'm sorry," Maria called out. The crystals in the sugar-white sand of Pensacola Beach glowed in the dark with a three-quarter moon hanging over the Gulf of Mexico. She gathered the grains in her hands and let the sand spill through her fingers. Had she lost her angel tonight?

Her heart felt heavy in her chest. Was it a sin to kiss an angel? He had kissed her head several times before and nothing happened. Except of course, the pleasure she received by feeling loved by her angel. Then the thought of his recent kiss sent pulses of sensations throughout her body once more.

Her lip felt swollen now and she ran her fingers across her mouth. Oh, she must look hideous after dealing with the thug on Tarragona Street. She was going to need ice to reduce the swelling. Her nurse's training came back to her, but did no good, since she was stranded on the beach. She would rather be stranded in Mike's arms. At least that way, nothing more could happen to her, except maybe being loved by an incredibly sexy angel.

• • •

Mike hovered as a spirit over María, his hands fisted at his sides. The evil spirits had been relentless in their pursuit of her. If he had finished them off quicker, the drug dealer would not have caught up with her. But then, the drug dealer was in no position to hurt anyone else for a while. Mike hadn't realized how easy it was to break human bones. He would have to remember his strength was greater than that of man.

He had almost lost control of himself when he kissed María. His body was flooded with emotions and sensations he had long ago forgotten. The thought of what he wanted to do to her not only lifted his spirits but had the two of them hovering over the sand. He barely remembered thinking himself here on the beach moments before he was lost in her embrace.

It had felt good to hold her and kiss her. She belonged in his arms. But the tightening of his groin made him realize how much he wanted her as a woman. Knowing María wanted him equally as much lulled him into satisfying his desires, a mistake he couldn't afford to make.

It was bad enough keeping evil spirits away from María but having to fight his own temptations was new to him.

He called on his mentor, Pete, the one spirit who could guide him through this. The one who had trained him.

Instantly, Pete appeared before Mike, hovering as well, and dressed in his battle regalia.

"I…kissed her, Pete, and I enjoyed it. I desire her. I'm fighting these temptations of the flesh, but—"

"You were once human, Mike. By manifesting in the flesh, you now feel as a human does. Humans are not the only ones with free will."

Mike glanced at Pete. *"What do you mean?"*

"Free will means you can choose between heaven and Earth, right and wrong. You can't have both. If you give in to your human passions, you will gain Earth but lose heaven."

"How do I fight this temptation?"

"Prayer." Then Pete left.

Mike watched María below as her disappointment and frustration showed in the way she pounded the soft sand with her fists. While he was in human form, the temptation to satisfy her need was great. As a spirit being, he felt concern and love for her. Angelic love was no comparison to the love humans felt for one another. Human love seemed to affect the whole body, not just the heart. Mike lowered himself to squat beside her.

Maria looked up. "I'm sorry. I was out of line," she said, lowering her gaze and releasing the sand trapped in her hands.

Mike ran his hand through her hair, loosening the soft, brown mane around her face. He loved the cool silkiness against his fingers. He lifted her chin, angling her face toward him. Seeing her bruises tugged at his heart.

"Hold still," he said as he gently caressed her swollen cheek.

She kept her trusting gaze locked on him as he ran the pad of his thumb across her lips, reducing the swollen mass to normal. He wanted to taste those lips, but he shook the thought from his mind. María had injuries that needed attention and he had to be strong.

Mike commanded a blanket into existence and spread it across the sand. "Sit here, while I heal you," he said.

María sat cross-legged on the pallet, still wearing her father's old suit pants and jacket, while Mike knelt in front of her. He touched a hand on both María's knees, closing his eyes in prayer. He gently caressed her knees, eliminating the bruises and repairing the skin, while avoiding her gaze. To feel her flesh against his hands would be nice, he thought. He was thankful she wore long pants. Besides, he wasn't entitled to that pleasure.

After removing her coat, he raised the sleeves of her shirt above her elbows, exposing her arms. She seemed so vulnerable as he inspected each forearm in turn, caressing the raw, scraped skin to normal. María closed her eyes and inhaled deeply. He could tell by her reaction that she enjoyed his touch. He wanted to give her more pleasure, but Pete's words came back to him.

"What you felt earlier, María, was normal," he began.

Her eyes flew open and grew wide.

"I…led you into temptation, and for that, I'm sorry," Mike said. He let out a breath he hadn't realized he was holding.

"You didn't tempt me, I tempted you."

Mike locked gazes with María. The truth was he wanted her as much as she wanted him. How could he comfort her without encouraging this strong desire within himself?

"Healing is one of my talents," he said, sitting next to her on the blanket when he finished.

"You promised to show me your other talents, as I recall." María nudged him with her shoulder. "Any time, any place, remember?"

He wrapped his arm around her, hugging her to him. It would be so easy to fulfill her desires now, as well as his own.

"Let's see, where should I start?" He scratched his chin. Before he could stop himself, his lips met hers with tenderness, as he took her to the ground. María opened her mouth to accept him and his kiss became demanding. Every fiber of his being caught fire. Instinct took over as he explored her mouth with his tongue. Maria clung to him, her arms pulling him closer. His body burned while his kiss devoured her. Twenty-three years of not feeling a woman in his arms awakened a sleeping passion that overwhelmed him.

Mike trailed kisses down María's neck and below her ear. Everything felt new yet very familiar to him. Her hand was in his hair, massaging his scalp and deepening his desire for her. Heat coursed through his veins as his erection hardened. When Maria moaned in pleasure, his eyes flew open and he pulled away.

"What's wrong? Why did you stop?"

"*This* is wrong," he said.

"You said my feelings were normal."

"Your feelings *are* normal. Mine are not."

Mike slid his arm out from under her and tried to move away. María grabbed his breastplate and held him in place.

"What are your feelings...exactly?" she demanded, glaring at him.

He saw the passion he had stirred up in her eyes. "I... I feel...overwhelmed." He ran a hand through his hair. "I want you, but that is not acceptable behavior for an angel. It's human behavior."

"You look pretty human to me, buster, and you feel human, too. Is it so wrong for you to kiss me?" María asked.

"Kissing you isn't the problem," he said. It was everything else he wanted to do to her. "Just as you have free will, so do angels. If I cross the line, I can't protect you anymore." He lowered his head. If anything should happen to María because he couldn't do his job, he wouldn't be able to forgive himself.

María hung her head in silence, leaning against Mike's shoulder.

Mike wrapped his arm around her, hugging her to him. It would be so easy to fulfill her desires, but he couldn't live with the consequences.

• • •

Finally, María turned away from him to lie down on the blanket. "Just disappear like you always do. I'll be all right by myself," she mumbled. She wiped at a tear that escaped down her cheek. It didn't matter who tempted whom, they both had wanted each other.

Mike's kiss had sent a confusion of emotions and heat coursing through her body, unlike anything she had experienced before. His touches had burned her, yet she wanted more.

He had said he was overwhelmed. Yes, that would explain her feelings as well. But if kissing an angel was a sin, what would be the consequences of going further?

María shook the thoughts from her mind. She had enough to deal with now as it was, like getting off the streets. Tonight had been harrowing. In the morning, she would hoof it back to Pensacola to report Tom's murder to Detective Anderson. Then she would do some research at the library to help Mike locate his family and get some closure on his past.

Next week, she would seek out a counselor at the Nursing Department because Mike was right, she needed help. The streets weren't safe anymore, especially after witnessing two murders in less than a week. Now the criminals were after her.

How could her life get so complicated? María's eyelids felt heavy. All she ever wanted was to be a nurse. She yawned. Now, even that dream seemed so far away. She closed her eyes and fell asleep.

• • •

When Mike thought María had fallen asleep, he fell back on the blanket, his arms folded behind his head. He had to fight these growing feelings. Besides, how would he protect María if he wasn't an angel? He glanced at her sleeping form. Would it be so difficult being human all the time?

Then he wondered what had caused his life to end so abruptly?

Chapter Six

He turned an evil eye on the injured man in the alley and recognized the handiwork of an angel.

"Hmmmm. I think I'll stick around awhile and stir up a little trouble," Beelzebub said before transporting himself to the home of Taylor Sanders.

• • •

"What do you mean?" Taylor Sanders yelled into his cell phone.

"Someone jumped Jembers while he was subduing the witness and broke his arm at the elbow. Never saw anything like it," Bannen said.

"Who was it?" Sanders demanded.

"Some guy with super-human strength. He tossed Jembers around like a rag doll. You know Jembers was a heavyweight wrestler?" Bannen said.

Sounds like the guy was on something. Beelzebub projected to Sanders.

"Was he a user?" Sanders asked.

"Don't know. I've never seen him before," Bannen replied.

"Well, clean up your mess. I don't want to have to investigate this," Sanders said. He closed his cell phone and raked a hand over his face.

You don't need this headache, Beelzebub projected. *It was the girl's fault. You'll have to get rid of her yourself.*

That's all Sanders needed, someone to come back and haunt him. He couldn't have any loose ends. Not when he was six months away from retirement.

Silently, Beelzebub watched as Sanders slept. Beelzebub waved his hand in the air and Sanders' slumber turned into a nightmarish dream.

Someone wants to put an end to your cash cow. You can't let that happen, Beelzebub suggested.

Sanders bolted upright from his bed, his skin clammy and moist with sweat. He glanced at his sleeping wife then got out of bed. He had to get some sleep. These nightmares had awakened him too many nights.

Beelzebub watched as Sanders stumbled into the bathroom, then took a sleeping pill.

More, take more, Beelzebub urged.

Sanders shook a couple more pills into his palm and hesitated, his hand trembling.

It would be easy to end this right now, Beelzebub suggested.

Sanders poured the extra pills back into the container and closed the lid. He swallowed his pill with water and climbed back into bed.

"Hmmmm, this will take some effort," Beelzebub thought, then disappeared.

• • •

While a spirit being, Mike required no sleep or food. In his human form however, he felt this heavy human body become sluggish when he didn't meet those needs, not to mention the other needs his body craved.

Mike closed his eyes and wrapped his arm around María's waist, cuddling behind her. Hours later, when he opened them again, the sun peeked over the horizon, painting the sky brilliant shades of rose, purple and gold.

María awoke with a start. She faced the Gulf of Mexico where a faint pinkish-orange glow erupted from the water. The soft lapping sound of waves washing ashore was followed by the sucking sound of the receding water. The salt air smelled good early in the morning and she preferred it over the pungent aroma of stale garbage dumpsters.

Something heavy lay over her waist. Glancing down, she saw an arm draped over her body. Her heart skipped a beat as she abruptly turned to face the owner.

Mike! She had forgotten how she got here.

"Sleep well?" he asked.

"Yes, actually, I thought I'd be cold, but I was comfortable all night."

"I surrounded us in warmth. The air is actually chilly now, but you're not exactly equipped for that kind of weather."

How she missed the comforts of a real home. Someday, she would be off the streets for good. But how much longer would she have to endure this?

Mike wrapped his arms around her, cuddling close.

"Hmmm. I'd love to wake up like this every morning," she said, feeling an overwhelming desire to kiss him.

"One day, María, your prayer will be answered," he said, moving a strand of hair away from her eyes. "Come, let's walk."

Mike helped María to her feet, and they walked toward the sunrise, holding hands in silence.

The chilled air mixed with the salty breeze had a crispness that only fall knew. María glanced at the waves rushing to shore. No one could take away her memories of Mike, even if she never saw him again. How much longer would she get to experience his warmth or look at that sexy smile? She silently thanked God for sending Mike to her.

The two of them walked along the beach, Mike in his battle dress and María with her pant legs rolled up. She splashed in the cold October surf of the Gulf of Mexico, while Mike held her hand.

Occasionally, María would stoop and pick up an interesting seashell, pocketing it in her father's old suit coat. Even Mike found a few unique shells.

Although Mike could transport them back to downtown Pensacola with the speed of thought, she relished their time together. If only it didn't have to end.

An hour and a half later, the two of them made it to the fishing pier on Pensacola Beach.

"We'll have to cross the bridge," she said, stopping to put on her shoes.

"I have a better idea," Mike said, pulling her toward him. He leaned against a light pole as he wrapped his arms around her. She held onto him and in the next instant, they were in front of the Pensacola Police Department. She reluctantly let go of him and realized how comfortable she felt with Mike.

"This sure beats riding the bus," she said. Walking up the steps, she remembered why she was here, Big Tom.

"I'm here to see Detective Anderson," she said to the officer at the desk.

"Detective Anderson is off today, can someone else help you?"

Remembering Detective Sanders sent a cold chill up her spine. "When will Anderson be back?"

"Monday."

"I'll come back," she said. She would call Anderson at home. Big Tom had waited long enough. She had to tell someone, and Mike seemed to think Anderson was okay.

Outside, on the steps of the police department, María spied a telephone booth across the street. Digging into her oversized pockets, her fingers found the change she needed to make the call.

"Detective Anderson?"

"Yes?"

"This is María Rojas. I'm calling about another murder." She explained everything that happened the night before, including her near-death experience at the killer's hand, and the fact that Mike incapacitated the man responsible.

"You two may want to stay away from the Square for a while," Anderson said.

No kidding. "Yeah," she agreed.

"I've got to make some calls. There's another detective I trust that's working today. Meet me Monday morning at the Police Station," he said. "Nine o'clock."

"I can't. I'm working until 2:30 pm."

"I'll come to you, then." Anderson hung up.

• • •

Taylor Sanders awoke with sweat beading up around his forehead, another nightmare about Ryan. Even the sleeping pill couldn't stop the dreams. He ran his hand through his damp hair. Why was he having these nightmares after twenty-three years anyway?

Sanders glanced over at his wife, Emily, who was still asleep. The slit in the drapes indicated daylight outside. He tossed the covers off and stood up, yawning. Coffee would wash away these nightmares. He grabbed his cell phone off the nightstand and headed for the kitchen.

Pulling the pot from the coffeemaker, Sanders realized it had been the same dream each time. He turned on the faucet and filled the carafe.

Ryan had faced the mole he suspected was dealing on the streets. Sanders sneaked up behind Garrett, the mole, and grabbed him. As Ryan approached cautiously, Sanders raised Garrett's gun hand. With a little pressure, the weapon fired, and the bullet hit Ryan in the throat. Then Sanders pushed Garrett away.

"You shot my partner," he said, then fired the fatal round into Garrett's chest.

As Sanders replaced the pot on the coffeemaker, flicking the switch, the memories of the final scene came back to him. Ryan's eyes were filled with shock, as Ryan slowly fell backward to the ground. The wound to Ryan's carotid artery took seconds to end his life.

If Ryan hadn't died that night, Sanders wouldn't be sitting on his nest egg now. The salary he got from the police department wasn't enough for the lifestyle he wanted. Soon, he and Emily would both retire and travel the globe.

Another thought occurred to him as he waited for the coffee to finish brewing. The girl had seen too much. If she hadn't already spilled her guts to Anderson, he could finish her off and make it look like an accident. Then again, maybe she hadn't told him a thing.

• • •

María walked with Mike to the Waffle House on Ninth Avenue.

"My favorite place to eat," he said, hugging her.

"Yeah, well, maybe we can change that," she said, entering the door he held open for her.

Once inside, María realized Mike had changed clothes again.

"I wish I could do that," she said.

"What?"

"Think on a different set of clothes whenever I wanted."

He smiled with a strange look on his face.

"What are you thinking?" she asked.

"How nice you would look in a bathing suit right now."

"Uh, no." She teased back. Looking around, she realized Susan wasn't there.

"It's later in the morning, so she's not here," Mike said.

"Are you remembering things about your past?" she asked.

"Yes. Some things are coming back, but in pieces."

"Well, after breakfast we'll go to the library and see what else we can find out about your life history."

When the waitress showed up, María found she had worked up an appetite from her hike on the beach. "Two All-Star Specials," she said, "with coffee."

After the woman left, María reached across the table and touched Mike's arm. "Why did God take both of my parents?" She asked.

"It was their time to go."

"He didn't have to make them both sick," she argued.

"Your father brought on his own death by his smoking, and you know that. The doctors had told him to quit more than once."

"My mother didn't make herself sick with pneumonia. She had taken care of others who were sick."

"Your mother missed your father very much, but she never told you."

"How did you know that? Did you read her mind, too?"

"Her Guardian Angel told me. When she got sick, she just gave up."

"My mother wasn't a quitter." María tapped the table with her finger.

"No, she wasn't. But the burden of his bills, her overworked schedule, and your schooling was too much for her to keep up with along with her cold. When it settled in her lungs, she thought more about your father and being with him. Everything else seemed insignificant. He had visited her before she died."

María's eyes welled up with tears. "Did she see him?"

"Yes, that's when she gave up. It was her time to go."

María's throat tightened at the thought that her parents were reunited but saddened at the thought that she had been orphaned.

"You are a strong person, María. Your strength lies inside you and your faith. If your parents hadn't died when they did, you wouldn't become the person you were meant to be."

Mike touched her cheek and calmness engulfed her, just as the waitress brought their food.

. . .

After their meal, María slid her arm through Mike's and walked toward the bus stop.

"Where are we going?" Mike asked.

"To the library."

"Then why are we going this way?"

"Because the bus stop is over there," she pointed.

"My way is faster," Mike said wrapping his arms around her. María held on tighter this time. What they found at the library may change her relationship with him and it saddened her.

When she opened her eyes, they were standing on the steps of the library. Mike kissed her head. "Our relationship can only grow stronger, María. That's a promise."

She looked up into those deep brown eyes, while her own misted over. She nodded while her throat tightened. She truly wanted to believe that.

Within minutes, they were inside the library, heading for the computers. María got online and began a search for newspaper articles for the year he was born. When she found what she was looking for, she made notes, then pulled Mike in front of the screen so he could read the articles.

Standing beside him, she chewed her nails, while reading the articles over his shoulder. All but one article seemed similar to what Susan had showed them.

"…although the evidence appears to corroborate Detective Sanders' story, foul play has not been ruled out," Mike read aloud.

"Here's another one." María pointed to the screen.

"Mysterious House Fire Claims Two," Mike read the title. "Mysterious house fire early Saturday morning claimed the life of Leah Ryan and her infant son. Ryan was the wife of slain police officer Mike Ryan." Mike sat silently staring at the screen.

The article gave information about the funeral, which María jotted down. "Here's another article, Mike," María scrolled down a little on the screen.

"It's a birth announcement; Kenneth Ryan, born September 3, 1996 at Sacred Heart Hospital. Oh, my gosh! That's the day you died," she said.

Mike glanced at María. "Leah must have gone into labor when she heard the news. That's why I didn't remember a son, or even having a child."

María put her hand on Mike's shoulder. "I'm really sorry, Mike." Mike covered her hand with his.

"I know where they are now," he said, his expression sad. He stood and headed for the door with María quickly following.

• • •

Mike stood out in the sunshine, praising God for the brief time he had with Leah. He only had good memories of her, and the Lord showed him that Leah and the child did not suffer. They had been pulled from the fire but had died of smoke inhalation.

Another thought occurred to him as María approached. He had known María for twenty-two years; far longer than he'd known Leah. He knew everything about María, even her intimate thoughts.

"Are you okay?" she asked, putting her arm around his waist.

Mike nodded and put his arm around María's shoulder. Since he had been a spirit being, he had had no time to mourn for Leah and the baby. He didn't feel sad learning about their deaths. Instead, he felt relief, knowing what happened, and finding closure on that aspect of his life.

Reading about the death of his and her parents did not sadden him either, for there was nothing he could do about it. The Lord had shown him they were all together in heaven.

"Memories coming back?" María asked.

"Yes, all but one."

CHAPTER SEVEN

Guilt washed over María as she thought about her behavior the night before. Mike had been married, and he had loved his wife, not to mention his son. She practically threw herself at him.

Shame mixed with guilt. He was an angel and she had tried to seduce him. What had gotten into her? She had never thrown herself at any man like that. Then again, no one ever affected her quite like Mike did.

She had to remember that he was just a figment of her imagination. He wasn't real.

Mike pinched her arm.

"Ouch! Why did you do that?" María demanded.

"That felt real, didn't it?"

"What are you talking about?"

"Just because I'm a spirit being doesn't make me any less real than that pinch I gave you."

Suddenly, María realized Mike had heard all her thoughts. Her face burned from embarrassment.

Mike pulled her close and kissed the top of her head.

"I have a lot of questions myself, María, just like you. I'm confused about my…feelings. Sometimes I think I should remain in spirit form, so I won't feel as humans feel. But I'm intrigued by all of this and the fact that memories come back more often while I'm in human form. I'm curious to see if I can remember my past, as well as my… final days."

María locked gazes with Mike. She knew then that she would do whatever it took to help him discover what ended his life, as long as she could keep him near her.

• • •

Memories flooded Mike's brain. Memories of his life before Leah as well as with her were now falling into place. He thought of the heartache both her parents and his own must have gone through over the loss of their children.

He had seen María making notes while he read the articles. He couldn't bring himself to look up his parents. Not yet. He needed to know how his life ended.

Was he a good cop? He would not have been an angel if it were otherwise. Most importantly, why was he given this chance to see his past?

Pieces of a larger puzzle were starting to fit and María seemed to play a key role in all of this. Could it be that God had designed this from the beginning, knowing that Mike would be her Guardian Angel? If he hadn't been, then he would never have seen his past. Mike would have gone on about his business of protecting someone else, never knowing he had been human.

All these feelings he had for María were real, but was falling in love with her God's design as well?

Mike was privileged to have known her so intimately for so long. He loved everything about her, yet he couldn't have her; not as a man would have a woman. Yahweh wasn't a cruel God. Everything had a purpose.

One day, perhaps, God would reveal his purpose for all of this in his timing. Mike offered up a prayer of thanksgiving.

• • •

"I thought we could go downtown and help Betty with her baskets," María said.

"Oh, yes, Saturday. I had forgotten," Mike responded.

"You looked far away," she said. Had she begun to lose him?

Mike lifted her chin with his finger. "I had been thinking about all the information we discovered."

"I got the location of the cemetery when you're ready for it," she offered. She wasn't sure he was ready to actually visit the graves of his wife and son just yet. Mike hadn't mentioned his parents, either, but she had jotted their names down, anyway.

The bus pulled up and they climbed aboard. María let Mike sit next to the window. Hopefully, more memories would be triggered as they rode to the laundromat.

Saturdays were laundry days. That's where María had met Betty. Betty ran the laundromat and would let María change clothes there and dry clean her father's suit and wash her undergarments in exchange for helping Betty make baskets.

She had gotten good at weaving baskets into an egg shape. Betty had been trying to get enough baskets made for the annual Seafood Festival that was coming up in November.

"I'm sure Betty will be glad to have the extra help with the baskets," María said as Mike stared out the window.

Mike turned to face her, taking her hand in his and giving it a squeeze. "Betty is lucky to have you as a friend." He winked.

His touch warmed her. She felt comfortable around Mike. What would she do without him? The bus pulled to a stop near the laundromat and they both got off.

"You're early today," Betty said, folding sheets.

"I had an adventure this morning, Betty," María began. She introduced Mike and told Betty about their walk along the beach.

"Mike's going to help us with the baskets today," she announced as she went into the bathroom to change into a long shirt and a pair of shorts she had in her zip-lock bag.

María took what few valuables she had out of her coat and put them into Betty's drawer in the office. She took the suit next door to the one-hour dry cleaners, then went back to wash her 'undies'.

"So how did you two meet?" Betty asked when they sat down to weave the baskets.

María glanced at Mike for his reaction. "I…met Mike near Tarragona Street. It was quite by accident."

"You can tell her the truth," Mike said, glancing at Betty, then María.

"You sure?"

Mike nodded.

María explained everything to Betty from the time of Joe Blue's murder to Big Tom's demise.

Betty made the sign of the cross. "Oh my God! I've never seen an angel before. I…expected…wings."

"Some have wings. Angels are spirit beings, just as you are, but you have a body. We can move through space and time with just a thought," Mike explained.

Betty looked confused, so Mike continued. "Mostly, we are messengers of God. We live to do his will. Most people never see us. We can be an intuition to someone, or an insight or vision, or we can appear as humans or animals. In other words, we can change form at will. Angels can rescue people or give aid."

Mike reached out and touched Betty's shoulder.

"We can anoint you with calming peace."

Betty's expression changed as he touched her.

"Guardian Angels have different jobs or responsibilities than Archangels, Virtues, Dominions, or any of the other choirs."

María thought about what Mike had told them and realized how special her relationship with him was. In the back of her mind, however, she felt that it was all coming to an end somehow.

María finished her basket and went to change back into her father's suit, with her clean 'undies' tucked in the zip-lock bag inside her coat pocket.

Betty locked up and ushered them outside where it was dark. The three of them headed to the square. In the past, María had waited for Betty to catch her bus before finding a place to sleep, but not tonight.

A dark vehicle drove slowly around the square then stopped on the far corner.

"What is it?" Betty asked.

María noticed Mike had stiffened. "Suspicious vehicle," Mike replied.

María's gut tightened at the thought that maybe they were looking for her.

While they waited for the bus, the car crept slowly around the corner, closer to where they stood.

"Pray for help, María," Mike said.

"God send us a legion of angles to protect us, in Jesus' name I pray," she said.

"There're only two of them," Betty said. "Maybe we can take them."

Mike touched María's eyelids, and when she opened her eyes, she saw the square filled with angels. Some were dressed like Mike, others in long gowns resembling togas. Some had wings, others didn't. But all of them had shields. Some of them had swords, while others had spears. They moved toward her, Betty and Mike.

The car pulled up beside them.

"You folks need a ride?" someone from inside the car asked.

"No, we're good," María said.

The man inside the car studied her, then shook his head and drove off.

"They'll be back," Mike said.

"Did they see the angels?" María asked.

"No, but their evil spirits did and talked them out of staying."

Before the bus came, the car returned. This time, it came faster down street.

"It looks like they are going to hit us," Betty said.

The car barreled down the road in their direction.

"When I give the word, jump back out of the way," Mike said.

Betty and María watched as the automobile drew near.

"Now!" Mike yelled.

Betty and María jumped back off the sidewalk into the bushes. The car went up on the curb and a man jumped out swinging his arms.

He threw Betty to the ground, but Mike was on top of him, hammering him with his fists.

"Betty, are you all right?" María asked, bending down to check on her friend. Concern washed over her as she checked Betty's vitals. Betty had a pulse, but she was unconscious.

Angels came to minister to Betty, while María watched Mike fight with the man who jumped them. When he was unconscious, another man showed up. He reached for María, but she picked up a couple of rocks and threw them at him.

"You want to play rough, do you?" the man said.

"I don't want to play at all," she shouted. "Go away!"

He tried to grab her, but María found a small limb from one of the trees and swung at the man. She connected with his elbow.

"Ouch! Give me that," he said.

"Sure," María said, swinging the limb and aiming at his knee. Her pulse shot up. The man grabbed the limb before she could connect and yanked it from her hands.

Surprise and fear grabbed her as she looked for a way out.

The angels were with Betty and Mike was busy with the other man. María ran into the darkened park. Hopefully the angels would help her. She headed for a bench where most of the angels stood.

"Uh, where did you guys come from?" the man said.

María turned in time to see the man backing away as the angels pushed toward him. It was as if the angels grew bigger as well. Mike came up from behind the man and spoke to him, but María couldn't hear what he said.

The man ran off. The evil spirits that had come with the two men had been battling a throng of angels with swords.

Each time an angel stabbed an evil spirit, it exploded into black dust.

Mike appeared before her, and most of the angels disappeared. "Betty needs help," he said.

María ran back to Betty and checked her pulse once more. It was weaker now and she was still unconscious.

"Oh, God, help me help Betty," she blinked back the tears that had pooled in her eyes.

In the distance, María heard the sound of an ambulance. She looked around but didn't see Mike. The angels were gone, too. She held Betty's hand.

"It's going to be all right, Betty. Hang in there," she said, trying to convince herself.

When the ambulance pulled down the street where María and Betty were, María stood up and ran to the center of the street, flagging them down. The ambulance pulled to a stop. A paramedic jumped out.

"What's wrong?"

"She was knocked unconscious. I'm not sure if she hit her head. Her pulse was stronger a while ago, but it's getting weaker now."

"We'll take it from here," the paramedic said.

The other one joined him, and they worked quickly to secure Betty to a gurney and put her in the ambulance.

"Can I ride with you?" María asked.

"Sure." The paramedic motioned for her to come with him. Before climbing into the back of the vehicle, María looked around, but didn't see Mike anywhere.

Why would he disappear like that?

"How did you happen to come down this street?" María asked when she was inside.

The two men looked at each other and shrugged.

"Didn't you call us?" one of them asked her.

"No. I don't have a phone. We were attacked by two men in a car while waiting for the bus," she explained.

"Well, we got a call about a female injured in a scuffle."

"Where are the police?" María asked.

"They'll meet us at the hospital," the driver said.

When the vehicle pulled to a stop at Sacred Heart Hospital, María and one of the paramedics hopped out of the back of the ambulance. The driver came around and the two of them wheeled Betty into the emergency room as María tried to keep up.

She had been to this hospital before when her father died and then, when her mother got sick. Her mother had worked here until her death. A strange sadness overwhelmed her as she walked through the doors.

A nurse she had seen before, but didn't know, handed her a clipboard to fill out.

"I'm a friend of hers, but I don't know much about her, really. I couldn't even tell you her last name," María tried to explain.

"Wait here," the nurse said, leaving with the clipboard.

María turned around to see where the paramedics took Betty, but they were gone. Instead, two orderlies pushed her through a set of double doors.

If only Mike was here. Things were happening too fast and it was all her fault. Those men were looking for her and not Betty. And where did those men go? How would she explain all this? She would call Detective Anderson. Maybe he could do something.

CHAPTER EIGHT

Detective Anderson walked through the door of the emergency room.

"Thank God you're here," María said, relieved.

"What happened?" Anderson asked.

"My friend Betty and I were waiting for the bus when two guys tried to run us off the sidewalk," she began. Her hands shook as the vivid memory played over in her mind. *Tell him the truth.* She heard Mike's voice in her head.

She took Detective Anderson outside where they could be alone. "Do you believe in angels?" she asked him, nervously.

"Well, I've never seen one, but I believe they exist, why?"

María swallowed hard. "My Guardian Angel saved my life when I witnessed the first murder. He kept me from screaming that night."

Anderson raised an eyebrow.

"That man who was with me when I looked through the mug shots is my Guardian Angel." María's heart pounded in her chest, apprehension rising. *Keep going, you're doing fine,* Mike's voice came to her.

"When he's in the flesh, he remembers things."

"What do you mean, 'in the flesh'?" Anderson asked.

"Well, when he manifests himself in the flesh, he has memories of his past…he used to be a police officer—"

"Mike Ryan! I knew he looked familiar," Anderson interrupted.

"We did some research today and found out about his death, along with his wife and child, but he doesn't remember how it happened."

Anderson ran a hand through his hair. He looked up then back to María. "I can't believe this is happening." He paced back and forth a couple times.

"Believe it," she whispered.

Suddenly, Mike stood before them and Anderson jumped back in surprise.

"My God! It is you," Anderson said.

"No, I'm a Guardian Angel, not God," Mike said, grabbing Anderson's arms. "Until I manifested in the flesh to protect María, I didn't know I had ever been human."

"You look the same as you did twenty-three years ago. You haven't changed a bit," Anderson said. "I miss…our friendship," he said, softly.

"Mike said you two used to fish together," María said.

"Yes, we did. A lot," Anderson said, smiling.

"These men who are after María are tied in with the first murder, as well as Tom's murder," Mike said.

Anderson looked at both of them. "Why don't you tell me about Tom's murder, from the beginning." Anderson pulled out a pad and pen and took notes while María filled him in. Mike gave more information about the man he wrestled with and whose arm he broke.

"I'll check inside to see if anyone came in with debilitating injuries lately," Anderson said.

"And I'll check on Betty," María said, walking beside him.

As Anderson reached for the door, he stopped and turned to face María and Mike. "You know, I never felt good about the explanation that Sanders gave about that night. Something just didn't sit right with me," Anderson said.

"Always go with your gut instinct," Mike said. "It's usually your Guardian Angel trying to tell you something."

María rolled her eyes at him. He was right, though. It seemed as if every time she tried to fight that inner voice, something bad happened.

Anderson stopped at the nurse's station, while María and Mike checked on Betty.

Inside Betty's room, Betty lay peacefully asleep on the bed, her arms at her sides.

"I hate to wake her," María said, wringing her hands with worry.

"Why would you want to?" Mike asked.

"I'll have to be at work early in the morning, remember?"

"I'll get you to work on time. Staying here tonight would be more comfortable than sleeping on the street."

María glanced at the two chairs against the wall. They certainly didn't look comfortable to her. "Sleeping on the beach is my new preference," she said. *Especially if it involved Mike.*

Mike glanced at her and raised his eyebrow. "There are some benches in the waiting area," he said.

María checked back with the nurse.

"Will Betty be able to go home tonight?" she asked the burly woman at the desk.

"I'm afraid not, hon. We're running some tests now and we've got her under observation for the night. We still need information from her when she wakes," the nurse said.

María nodded.

Mike wrapped an arm around her shoulder to guide her to the waiting area.

"Sit here and I'll get us some coffee," Mike said.

"I thought you didn't have any money," she said.

Mike opened his hand and quarters filled his palm.

"Hey! How come you didn't do that before?" she asked, touching the coins.

"I didn't know I could until now," he said. Mike popped the coins into his pocket and headed for the vending machines.

Within minutes, Detective Anderson came and sat beside María.

"I want to thank you for that information, María," Anderson looked around the nearly empty room. "Where is he?" he whispered.

"Mike went to get coffee," she said.

"A gentleman was admitted last night with a broken elbow," Anderson began. "I've got a name and address. I'm heading back to the station to do some research tonight. Will you be at work in the morning?"

"Yes."

"Good. I'll come by there and fill you in."

Mike approached as Anderson stood to leave.

"Hey, buddy. We've got a lot of catching up to do, don't we?" Anderson said to Mike.

Mike nodded and handed María her coffee. "You are more helpful than you realize," Mike said.

"I know you want closure on your life as a police officer, Mike. I hope I can help you with that." Anderson shook Mike's hand and then headed out the door.

Mike had that faraway look in his eyes again, so María quietly watched from the seat beside him, sipping her coffee.

• • •

From the other side of Pensacola, Detective Sanders drove downtown, like Satan himself was on his tail.

"You don't need these people anymore," Beelzebub whispered in Sanders' ear. *"They can't do anything right. It's time you cut your ties with them. A meeting tomorrow night in the alley across from Rosie O'Grady's will be the perfect place to end this."*

Sanders flipped open his cell phone and hit the speed dial for Roberts. "Roberts? Sanders here. I need to set up a meeting tomorrow night."

"Why?"

"Something happened last night that we need to take care of."

"If you're talking about the incident with Jembers and Bannen, then yeah, we need to talk. You were supposed to keep the alley clear."

"The deal was to keep the heat off your people," Sanders said.

"The word on the street is the girl has ties to the heat and she's bringing it down on everyone."

"I'll take care of her, just be there tomorrow, midnight."

Sanders closed his phone. He would find that girl tonight. She had to be homeless to be in so many different places at the wrong time.

Sanders drove all over downtown Pensacola, checking alley after alley. She had to be here somewhere. By 4:00 am he got hungry and headed to the Waffle House on Ninth Avenue.

Susan was there. It was about time for her to retire, he thought, as he opened the door and walked inside.

"Hello, Detective. What'll it be this morning?"

"Eggs over medium, grits and sausage," he said as he sat down at his familiar corner booth. From there he could see everyone coming and going.

Susan poured his coffee and went back to the grill.

Sanders scratched his head. He had to find that girl tonight. There was too much riding on her to let it go.

Susan set his plate down and poured another cup of coffee.

"Have you seen the girl and the man who looked like my old partner?" Sanders asked her.

"Not in a while," she said. She hesitated at the table. "Have you got a business card?"

"Yeah, why?"

"Well, if I had your number, I'd call you when I *do* see her." Susan stood there, one hand on her hip and the coffee pot in the other hand.

Sanders reached into his billfold and pulled out a business card, handing it to her. "Be sure you call me the minute you see her. Day or night," he said.

"Sure," Susan said, sticking the card in her apron pocket. She turned and headed back to the grill.

When Sanders finished eating, he left a tip and headed out the door.

CHAPTER NINE

Shortly after 5:00 am, Mike stirred María from her slumber.

"It's time to head to the Greasy Spoon," Mike said.

María glanced at the clock. "Can't we wait another thirty minutes?" She yawned.

"I was hoping for breakfast at the Waffle House one last time," Mike said.

One last time? María sat up. *Does he know something he's not telling?* María arched an eyebrow. "Why did you say that?"

"I have a feeling things will be different after today," he said.

"A feeling?"

Mike nodded.

María stood and stretched. She didn't like the sound of that. Mike never mentioned feelings before. In fact, she was getting used to having Mike around. She didn't want to think of him not being here. "In what way will things be different?" she asked, walking next to Mike.

"I'm not sure."

María grabbed Mike's arm and stopped him in his tracks.

"You're not leaving me, are you?" Her heart fluttered at the thought, as a stab of pain shot through her heart.

Mike turned to face her. "You have a dream to become a nurse like your mother. My job is to protect you from harm and make sure you follow through and succeed with your dream. You promised me you would call the school and register for classes," he said, lifting her chin.

"I will. When I get my first break today, I'll make the call."

Mike put his arm around María as they stepped off the elevator to the downstairs lobby. Then, he flashed them to the Waffle House on Ninth Avenue and held the door for her.

"Well, I've been wondering what happened to you two," Susan said, greeting them at the door.

"Hello, Susan," María said, sliding into the corner booth with Mike.

Susan poured coffee for both of them. "Your old partner is anxious to find your friend, here," Susan said to Mike. She pulled a card out of her apron pocket and handed it to him.

Mike dropped the card instantly and wiped his hands across his pants legs.

"What's the matter?" Susan and María said in unison.

Mike glanced up at María, his eyes wide and a shocked look on his face.

María reached out and touched his arm. "What is it?" she whispered.

"I saw evil spirits when I touched the card, and I felt myself die," he said.

"Good Lord," Susan said, picking up the card by the corner. She carefully carried it to the grill area. María stood up to watch as Susan stuck the card in the flame from the grill. She kept it there several seconds. "This thing won't burn," Susan said.

"Let me see that," Bobby, the cook, said, pulling out a lighter. He held the lighter under the card for almost a full minute and the card would not catch fire.

"Beelzebub," Mike whispered.

"Who?" María asked.

"Satan."

María swallowed hard. "What has Satan got to do with that card?"

"He is behind the man whose name is on that card," Mike said.

Susan threw the card in the trash can when it wouldn't burn.

"But that was your ex-partner, Taylor Sanders," María said.

"Exactly."

Several long minutes later, Susan brought them their specials. Mike was quiet while he ate.

Later, Susan returned with the coffee. "You know, I remember how you died. No one should have to go through that twice," she said.

"I won't die again," Mike said, "but I may have to go through those feelings again to see how it happened.

María reached for his hand. "Is that what you meant earlier?" she asked.

"No. Things will be different between us," he said, his eyes full of sadness.

A great sense of foreboding overwhelmed her. She didn't want to lose Mike or his friendship. "Does it have to change?" she asked.

"It's inevitable."

• • •

Mike manifested money and paid for the meal. Afterward, he walked with María toward the Greasy Spoon. He wanted to savor this time with her. He didn't understand what was happening, but he knew, deep inside, that something was about to change.

By the time the two of them arrived at the restaurant, Mr. Brodsky was just opening the door.

"Good morning!" Mr. Brodsky said, holding the door for them.

"Good morning," María said as she and Mike stepped inside.

María changed into the uniform they had saved for her, while Mike put on his apron to prepare for the breakfast crowd.

Halfway through the breakfast shift, he saw Detective Anderson come in. Mike watched as María greeted him and escorted him to a table.

"Hi, Detective," María said, pouring his coffee. "What can I get you today?"

"I'll have two eggs over easy, bacon and toast," he said. María scribbled down the order, but before she could leave, Anderson reached for her arm.

"I found a nurse from the hospital who is willing to look at the mug shots for me, to identify the man with the broken elbow."

"Do you want me to take another look at the mug shots?" María asked. "Maybe I can pick out the man from last night."

"Sure, I can use all the help I can get," he said.

A few minutes later, María brought Anderson his food.

"Where do you go when you leave here, María?" Anderson asked, sipping his coffee.

"Some days I go to the bank, but mostly I hang out downtown until the Soup Kitchen opens. I go and help them set up and serve the food."

"Do you have a place to stay?"

"Not yet. I promised Mike I would call the college and see about getting back into the nursing program. I had to drop out when the landlord kicked me out. He has all my books and stuff. Maybe the counselor will know someone who is renting to students."

"What about tonight?" Anderson asked, picking up a slice of bacon.

María knew where she wanted to be and that was on the beach in Mike's arms. "I'm not sure yet," she said.

"Be sure and call me if you decide to look at the mug shots," Anderson said.

"I will." María turned and left. Anderson seemed like a nice guy.

She took some dishes into the kitchen for Mike to wash. "Anderson wants me to look at mug shots again," she said, handing the plates to Mike. "I think I'll take care of school first, then I can head to the police department."

Mike smiled at her as she turned to check on her customers. She had more customers today than yesterday, so her tips were a little better.

After the breakfast and lunch rush was over and María had cleaned up her area, she showered and changed into her father's old suit.

"Are you ready?" Mike asked, stacking the last of the dishes.

"Whenever you are," she said. She tucked her wet hair up under her hat.

The two of them headed to the bus stop. The blue sky was bright after they'd been inside a dark restaurant all morning, but the air was crisp and cool. Walking around with a wet head made her shiver from the dampness. She missed her hairdryer and all the comforts of home.

"Thank you for keeping your promise," Mike said, giving her a squeeze. She wanted to squeeze him back and kiss him, but the bus pulled up.

"Perfect timing," she whispered.

Mike grinned and ushered her up the steps.

Later, María stood outside the office in the nursing department, waiting to speak to a counselor. Mike sat on a chair, flipping through a magazine.

"What if they don't take me back?" she said, wringing her hands.

"Why wouldn't they?"

"Because I was gone a whole semester?"

"You were a good student, María. I don't think they would want to lose you."

"María Rojas?" The counselor called out to the room. María went inside with the counselor.

"Hello, María, I'm Terri Smith." She offered her hand and María shook it. "Have a seat."

"What can I help you with?"

"I…um…dropped out last semester after my mother died. I lost everything I owned when the landlord locked me out of my apartment. I owe him two month's rent to get my things back, but I want to finish school."

"Give me your student number, María, and we'll see what we've got."

•   •   •

Although Mike sat outside the office in the waiting area, his mind was with María. He could hear what the counselor said. He knew they would let her back into the program. It was her destiny. There were lives she would have an impact on in the future. Now if they could only help her find a place to live, he would have accomplished one of his missions.

A sadness washed over him, but he didn't know why, unless it had something to do with letting go of María. He should have never gotten this close to her. His human feelings were interfering with the Lord's work.

His second mission was to keep her alive so she could testify against the drug traffickers from the neighborhood.

Thirty minutes later, María came out of the counselor's office. Mike stood and walked with her down the hall and out the door of the building.

"Ms. Smith gave me a name of someone to contact about my mother's death. Apparently, this person has been trying to reach me through the college," María said.

"And what did she say about finishing the program?" Mike asked.

"I'm registered for the next semester. I can pick up where I left off, and my financial aid was still available."

Mike gave her a hug. "Did she give you a contact for a place to stay?" he asked.

"No, but she put me in the work study program. I start working at the hospital next week."

"Good for you!" Mike said, beaming.

"I told Mr. Brodsky today that I would be going back to school. I hope that gives him enough time to hire some new help."

"I'm sure he will find someone," Mike said as they headed to the bus stop.

"Once I get finished at the police station, I'll have enough time to get back to the Soup Kitchen and help with supper," María said. Then a thought occurred to her. "I need to check with Mr. Turner and find out the exact amount I owe him for my things. Maybe I can make payments."

"Hopefully, he will work with you," Mike said.

When they arrived at the police station, she spoke to the officer at the desk.

"I need to speak with Detective Anderson," she said.

"He's not here right now. He just left," the officer said.

"Can I borrow your phone?" she asked.

"There's a pay phone outside," he said.

Great. María ran out the door and dialed Anderson's number.

"Detective, I'm at the station if you want me to look over the mug shots," María said.

"I'm on my way back. Just wait for me," he said.

María looked up Turner's number and called him as well.

"Mr. Turner, this is María Rojas, the one you kicked out the day they buried my mother. I want my things back. How much do I owe you?"

"You owe me $800. I sold some of your things because I didn't think you were coming back," Turner said. "Now there's a storage fee on top of that."

"What do you mean, you sold some of my things? How could you? And I'm not paying a storage fee!"

"Well, you bring me the money and you'll get your stuff. I'm here seven days a week." Turner hung up the phone.

María squeezed the phone and went to bang it against the phone box, but Mike grabbed it from her. He cradled her in his arms and she calmed down immediately.

"Why does this stuff happen to me?" she cried out.

"Let's go inside," Mike said and ushered her toward the station.

When Anderson arrived, the three of them walked to the room where the books were kept.

"Have a look at these, Maria. Can I have a word with you, Mike?" Anderson asked. The two of them stepped out of the room for several minutes.

María got through the first book with no luck. Mike returned and looked over her shoulder. The second book, she hit pay dirt.

"That's him! That's the one whose arm you broke," María pointed.

Mike leaned over her shoulder. His face was so close she could kiss his cheek. She wanted to do more than that, but would God forgive her? Mike pulled back some and gazed into her eyes. *Don't tempt me, María.* Then he backed away from her.

She rested her elbows on the table and cradled her head in her hands. What was she thinking? He knew her thoughts. *I'm sorry.*

"See if you can remember the two who ran you and Betty down," Mike said.

María searched through another book before she found two who looked like her assailants.

Anderson came into the room with two Cokes.

"Thanks," Mike said. "You remembered."

"You used to drink these like they were water," Anderson said. He smiled at the thought.

"I remember that," Mike chuckled, then took a swig of his drink.

María stared at Mike. She wanted to keep him for herself. How was she going to let him go? Then again, how could she stop him? She cleared her throat and showed the images to Anderson.

"I know this guy," Anderson pointed at the first one. "I've arrested him several times. You did good, María." Anderson patted her arm. "This is the same one the nurse identified."

"What happens now?" she asked.

"I'll follow up on the other two and get warrants out for all three of them," he said. "Where are you two headed now?"

"We're headed to the Soup Kitchen to help out and then I eat there," she said.

"You keep me posted on your whereabouts," he said.

"Okay. I'll just sleep in the—"

"We'll be heading to the beach tonight, where it's safer," Mike said.

CHAPTER TEN

As María and Mike headed to the Soup Kitchen, she felt someone following them. She turned to look several times, but no one was there.

"Do you feel it?" she asked Mike.

Mike glanced at her. "Yes. He's on foot about fifty yards behind us," he said.

"Should we run?" she asked.

"No. I won't let anything happen to you, María, you know that."

"I know," she said, wrapping her arm through his. She felt safe with him. When they reached the Soup Kitchen, Mike remained in the flesh.

"You're coming inside tonight?" María smiled.

"Yes." Mike smiled back and gave her hand a squeeze.

María and Mike helped set up the tables and chairs. Then when the people started filing in, they helped dish out the soup. Finally, after things slowed down, María filled a bowl for Mike and herself, while Mike brought the tea to the table.

"When I told Mr. Brodsky that I would be going back to school," she began, "he gave me my last paycheck today." She stopped eating and pulled the envelope out to open it.

Her breath caught in her throat when she saw the money and a business card.

"What is it?" Mike asked, holding his spoon over his bowl.

"He gave me a $100 bonus," she said. She wiped at her eyes and studied the card. Mike handed her a napkin.

"Tomorrow I'll see Mr. Turner," she said, patting her eyes dry.

"Call the woman who has been trying to reach you," he said.

María nodded. She had almost forgotten that. When they finished eating, María and Mike helped clean up.

"I don't start my new job until next week, but now I have a contact to call about a room at the YWCA."

Mike nodded. He knew his time in the flesh would come to an end. María was on her way to completing her nurse's training. He had grown fond of her all this time. He would miss her touch. He inhaled her scent while she clung to him as they walked out the door.

The night was chilly. Mike put his arm around María's shoulders and she slid her arm around his waist. They had walked a block toward the square when a car came down the road at a slow pace, its lights off. Mike tightened his hold on María.

When they passed an alley, Mike heard the distinct sound of a gun being cocked.

"Well, well, look what we have here," Taylor Sanders said, gazing at María. "The streetwalking troublemaker."

Mike pushed María behind him. "She's not a street-walker, Taylor. The only trouble she's seen has been caused by you," Mike said.

"How do you know my name?" Sanders asked.

Mike stepped out under the glow of the street lamp.

Sanders gasped. "You can't be! I…killed you twenty-three years ago."

"Yes, you did. I remember it now. I confronted one of your…associates about his drug deals. I think you came from the back of the alley, telling him to hold it. You made me believe you had your gun on him, but when you moved closer, you pulled his gun hand up and squeezed the trigger, shooting me in the throat."

"You had no right butting in on my cash cow. All I had to do was keep the cops away from the drop points and I made a little money. But you just about blew my cover. I had to get rid you. What are you…a ghost?"

"No, Taylor, I'm an angel."

"Yeah, right."

"What happened to Mike's wife?" María asked, peeking out from behind Mike.

"I didn't know how much you had told her," Sanders said, glancing at Mike, "so I had to get rid of her, too." Sanders shrugged.

"You cold-blooded murderer!" María shouted.

"You killed my son," Mike said. "He never had a chance in this world."

"How did you know about that? You were dead when he was born," Sanders said.

"Put on the armor of God, María," Mike whispered over his shoulder.

María recited the Ephesians verse she had memorized years ago. When she glanced up, she and Mike were surrounded by evil spirits. They were black, eerie shadows that hovered around Sanders and another man who came up from behind him.

María wore a suit of armor, covering her body head to toe, much like what a knight would wear. In one hand, she held a wide, heavy sword. In her other hand was a large shield.

"God, send us a legion of angels to surround us, in Jesus' name I pray," she said. Before she could raise her sword, more angels than she could count battled the evil spirits, along with Mike.

María held up her shield as fiery darts flew at her. Sanders made a move toward her and she wielded the sword with ease. He jumped back.

"Shoot them!" Sanders' accomplice yelled.

Mike jumped in front of María and caught the bullet in his chest.

"No!" María yelled.

"Hold it right there, Sanders!" a familiar voice yelled from behind her. Anderson, along with a dozen uniformed officers surrounded Sanders and the other man.

When Sanders dropped his gun, María dropped her sword and shield and ran to Mike. He lay unconscious on the ground.

"Mike! Wake up. Mike, don't leave me. I need you," she said, feeling for a pulse. It was weak.

Glancing up, María noticed the angels moving toward her. Without much effort, they lifted Mike and carried him off to heaven as his body faded into a spirit being.

There, on the ground, were wires attached to small, circular pads. Had Mike been wearing these? She picked them up, intending to ask Anderson. The evil spirits had fled and some of the angels remained in the alley on guard.

María felt the presence of someone behind her. She swung around and saw a tall blond man standing there, his hand on her shoulder. "Are you my new Guardian Angel?" she asked.

He nodded.

María's throat tightened at the thought of losing Mike. She shouldn't have kissed him. *Oh, God, I'm sorry I kissed your angel. Please forgive me. Don't punish Mike for that. It wasn't his fault.*

Anderson patted María on the other shoulder. María glanced at Anderson, handing him the set of wires. Two officers led Sanders and the other man off toward the patrol cars, both in handcuffs.

"Are you all right?" Anderson asked.

Her heart in her throat; all she could do was nod.

"Where are you staying tonight?" Anderson asked.

"I…don't know." A tear fell down her cheek.

"I'll take you to the station while I process these guys, then I'll put you up in a hotel for a couple of nights," he offered.

María nodded. "Did you see what happened to Mike?" she asked. She didn't know if she could explain it otherwise.

"We…all did." He put his arm around her and walked her to the car.

There was no sign of a body or blood, but Sanders had shot his gun. Dazed, María got into Anderson's car.

Later, at the station, she sat near the coffee pot, drinking and waiting for Anderson. When he finished a couple hours later, he drove María to a nearby hotel and paid for a room for her for a couple days.

"I start my new job at the hospital on Wednesday, but tomorrow I'll call the YWCA about a room."

"Good. You know I'll need you to testify about what happened here tonight, right?" Anderson asked.

María nodded.

"Now, if you need anything, just call me," Anderson said.

"Well…" María remembered her dilemma with Mr. Turner. "There is something I need advice on," she said. María then explained her situation with Turner.

"When you're ready to get your things, call me. I'll escort you to the property."

"Thanks. Um, Detective, how am I going to explain Mike?" she asked.

"I'm not sure, but thanks to Mike, we have Sanders' confession on tape. This will implicate Sanders in Mike's murder twenty-three years ago."

• • •

Two days later, María moved into her new room at the YWCA. She called Detective Anderson and gave him the phone number. He agreed to pick her up so she could get her things from Mr. Turner.

• • •

"Well, you got here just in time. I was about to sell the rest of this stuff to get my money," Turner said.

"You had no right!" María said.

"I can do whatever I want since you owe me back rent," Turner said.

"How much does she owe you?" Anderson asked.

"Who are you?" Turner asked, glaring at him.

"Detective Anderson, from the Pensacola Police Department," he said, whipping out his ID and badge.

"Hey, I did nothing wrong," Turner said, raising his hands in surrender.

"I asked you how much does she owe?" Anderson said.

"She owed $800 in back rent for two months, plus the storage fee of all her things," Turner said.

"This is your storage unit?" Anderson asked. María and Anderson stood in front of a small room at the end of the apartment building. The room contained tools, a riding lawn mower, weed trimmers, and clippers, along with boxes of things and odds and ends of furniture that looked familiar.

"Yes," Turner said.

"What do you say to dropping the charge for storage and giving her the rest of her things, and she won't charge you with theft," Anderson said.

"I didn't steal her stuff," Turner said.

"You are entitled to your money, Mr. Turner, but you are not entitled to deny her access to her things. She did not abandon her belongings. You denied her access to them. Now that is stealing, especially given the fact that you sold her things for profit."

Turner looked uneasy.

"How much did you make on the sale of her things?" Anderson asked.

Turner scratched his stubble. "I'd have to look it up."

"You do that." Anderson looked at his watch. "We have a few minutes."

Turner went inside his apartment, which was beside the storage room. Within minutes, he came out and handed Anderson a copy of a receipt from his pad.

"Two hundred and seventy five dollars," Anderson said, showing María the receipt.

"What did you sell?" María demanded.

"Your sofa, coffee table, chairs, and some men's clothes."

María rubbed her face with her hands. "Where are the bedroom and dining room furniture?" María asked.

Turner clenched his jaws. He pulled another receipt off the pad and handed it to her.

"Three hundred and fifty dollars?" María shouted. "You had the nerve to sell my things and demand that I pay you $800 for back rent?"

Turner shrugged. "It was in my way. I needed the room and you owed me money. I didn't know if I'd ever get it back," Turner said.

"Did it ever occur to you to ask her for payment, or work with her on it?" Anderson asked.

"I spoke to her mother about it, but she didn't get back to me," Turner said.

"My mother was sick with pneumonia. She died, Mr. Turner. I didn't know about her finances. You had the nerve to kick me out the day of her funeral. You have no heart at all." María choked at the words.

Anderson put his arm around her. "You forced her to live on the street, Mr. Turner. She dropped out of school because you kept all her books and things. She's a nursing student. You deprived her of her education as well."

"I didn't know," Turner said with his head down.

"I suggest you get to know your tenants, Mr. Turner. Be more humane in the future," Anderson said.

"Do you still have my books?" María asked.

"Everything else is in the back, here," Turner pointed.

María pulled out her bonus money from Mr. Brodsky along with some money she took out of the bank and paid

Turner in cash for the difference. "I want a receipt," she said.

Turner moved the mower out of the room and helped María and Anderson load some of her things into Anderson's car.

"We'll be back this afternoon with a small trailer and pick up the rest of her things," Anderson said, when they couldn't get another thing in his car.

"Detective, I owe you so much. I'm…grateful for your help," María said.

"He would have taken advantage of you, María. I'm glad I could help. I've got a small trailer at my house and an SUV. I'll stop by later this afternoon, when I get off and help you with the rest of your things."

"Thanks, Detective," María said after he had helped her unload her stuff at the YWCA.

She spent the afternoon unpacking her clothes and books, and sorted through the things she couldn't keep. The Y was planning a yard sale for the end of the month, so she donated her mother's clothes. She kept the little table for a desk and the small bookcase for her books.

After her second trip with Anderson, her room looked a little more "homey" and the Y had a few more items for the yard sale. Losing a lot of her things had hurt, but her life was turning around for the better. Once she started working as a nurse, she would be able to start over with new furnishings, and that was her only comfort. She managed to save a few mementos of her parents, along with the scrapbook her mother had kept up over the years.

María had tried not to think about Mike, but he had been so much a part of her life lately, that she felt a void in her heart. It was comforting to know she still had a

Guardian Angel, but it wasn't the same. She did communicate with him from time to time, though.

• • •

Waking up in the morning on a comfortable bed and fixing herself a small breakfast brought back thoughts of Mike and the Waffle House.

While waiting for the bus, she smiled at the thought of Mike's dark, curly hair and that dimple in his left cheek. She had to get her mind off him and onto other things.

Once she arrived at the hospital, she found Mrs. Whitmer in emergency.

"You'll be working in Central Supply," Mrs. Whitmer said. "You'll need scrubs to work in, and you'll bring supplies to the ER and other departments as needed. Everything they use they order from CS and then you will bring it to those departments," Whitmer explained.

Whitmer gave María a tour of the hospital, while explaining her duties. "Can you start in the morning?"

"Yes, I'll be here," María said.

Mrs. Whitmer excused herself and María found her way out the door. She would have to shop for scrubs. The money she had saved from paying Mr. Turner would cover that expense.

• • •

Months later, as María adjusted to her class load and working in Central Supply, she had just gotten off from work as an ambulance pulled up at ER. María stood back, out of the way and watched as two EMTs jumped out from the back and pulled a gurney through the doors. The dark-headed EMT caught her attention and brought back thoughts of Mike.

She headed out the door toward the bus stop nearby. By the time she was halfway there, the two EMTs returned to the ambulance with the gurney. She glanced at the dark-headed man once more and he turned to look at her. Her heart skipped a beat when he smiled. Was that a dimple on his left cheek? She ran back towards the vehicle. "Mike?"

The man said something to his partner, then ran toward her.

"Mike!" María shouted as he embraced her and swung her around. She pulled back slightly. "I thought you were dead," she whispered.

"I was. God heard your prayer, María, and asked if I wanted to remain in heaven as an angel, or return to Earth as a human."

María swallowed hard. "He made you choose between heaven and Earth?"

"I wanted a second chance at life…with you, María," he said. He kissed her passionately on the lips.

María wanted more of this, but not here in the parking lot where she worked. "Hmmm." She pulled away slightly. Looking up, she uttered, "Thank you, God!" María gazed into Mike's eyes. "You're not a cop anymore?"

"No. I had been killed as Mike Ryan, who was a cop. Now, I'm Mike Angelo, an EMT." Mike's arms were still around María, pressing her against him. "God gave me the gift of healing while I was an angel, so I asked to be in the health field where I could put it to good use."

"Perfect. Does this mean we can…be together?" she asked hesitantly.

"After your graduation, I'd like to marry you, if you'll have me," he said.

"Are you kidding? Why wait until graduation?" she asked.

"It will give me time to save up for a home for the two of us. Besides, you need to study."

"How can I study thinking about you?" María asked.

Mike hugged her tight. "We'll work on that together."